COURAGE, 30,000 BC

THE BOQUEIRÃO REFUGE AT PEDRA FURADA

BONNYE MATTHEWS

Award Winning Writer
of Prehistoric Fiction

PUBLICATION CONSULTANTS
PUBLISHING THE WORKS OF AUTHORS WORLDWIDE

PO Box 221974 Anchorage, Alaska 99522-1974
books@publicationconsultants.com—www.publicationconsultants.com

ISBN 978-1-59433-687-4
eISBN 978-1-59433-688-1

Library of Congress Catalog Card Number: 2017931908

Cover attribution:
Young girl: Author, Pedro França/MinC CCA 2.0
Mimosa tree: Public Domain
Crocodile: Author: Tomás Castelazo CCA-SA 2.5

Manufactured in the United States of America.

Acknowledgement

Without the assistance of several people this book would not be. These people are my brother, Randy Matthews, and then Sally Sutherland, Patricia Gilmore, Robert Arthur, Pat Meiwes, and Rebecca Goodrich. Each contributed far in excess of what could be expected or hoped for based on family, friendship, or love of reading. I also thank my publisher, Evan Swensen, who had the courage to take on this project.

Exordium

I received an invitation from the storyteller, Muz. I accepted. I always accept. In my hurry I snatch a plush throw and slide it around my shoulders to avoid the night's chill. At the campfire I sit and eagerly prepare to listen to his weaving a new Place History. His voice is deep, resonant. Each word is crafted carefully, spoken with crystal clarity. Muz holds attention magnetically so that I never wander from the story. Time stands still even while tiny red specks from the campfire rise to the darkness above. Muz is a bent-over, exceedingly wrinkled old man, bow-legged from old age, who wears a simple animal skin skirt, as worn as he is. The skirt dangles to his knees and sports a partial deboned tail on the side. The tail used to be a pouch but is no longer serviceable. Muz carries the scent of old dust, roses, or evergreens, depending on what he deems appropriate. His snarl-free, thin, weightless, waist-length hair is white and drifts freely in the breeze. He sees through his hair with obsidian black eyes riveting forward through wrinkled upper lids held at bay by thinning lashes. Nothing clouds his vision. Unlike me he is unaffected by the cool breeze.

I watch the images he creates between his gnarled, outstretched-towards-me hands, the backs of which display huge blue veins snaking across his thin skin. Muz displays the living earth between his hands. With time suspended, we travel to a period where he displays the great break-apart of South America from Africa. What a sight that break-apart is! It causes me to catch my breath!

He doesn't mention the river's flow, but rather Muz asks what I notice unusual about the image after the break-apart. That is how Muz causes me to learn. It takes a moment for me to spot the flow of the Amazon River from east to west, the reverse of what I'd expect. The break from Africa left the east coast of South America elevated. About 65 million years ago, the time of dinosaur extinction, the Andes Mountains began to form on the west coast of South America. They continued to grow. About 16 million years ago, when the mountains finally blocked the river's exit, the entire river changed from east to west into the present west to east flow to exit at last into the Atlantic Ocean. The docking of South America to North America occurred about ten million years later, and animals began to move between the Americas as they've been doing now for three million years.

Even before all that, in a geologic time called the Silurian from 443.8 million years ago to 419.2 million years ago, the place not time where this story occurs, the Serra da Capivara National Park was underwater, a sea floor in warm water. Over time the land rose to become what it is today. The composition is sandstone, a material that washes out easier than some rock, leaving behind places of refuge for land animals and people. Muz tells the story of environmental creation and change interwoven with a sharp focus on a tiny point in time and place. The people there create exceptional art, reflecting a vibrant community in the midst of great change, all in a place that is not easily accessed.

Time remains suspended. I walk through the story with him as he tells it. I can feel it, smell it, see it, touch it, taste it, sense it—I can be there. Now the campfire is reduced to white-edged cinders. Muz rises and leaves in an aura of golden light, entrusting me with this tiny part of the story to tell—the part about the people—a story from the past shared in the present for me to share for the future.

Dedication

I dedicate this novella specifically to the Toca do Boqueirão da Pedra Furada archaeological site, and generally to the Serra da Capivara National Park in Brazil where the site is located. According to Nième Guidon, the lead archaeologist associated with the park, people began to occupy the specific location somewhere between 48,700 and 32,000 years ago. She maintains that people were in the area for 100,000 years. The Bradshaw Foundation dates the artwork at the site at between 36,000 to 25,000 years ago. Clovis-First believers argue about the dates and claim the artifacts are natural objects. Time will tell.

In the images that follow, you can see what I have seen as I entered the world Muz presented. This is an enchanted place. Pedra Furada means **pierced stone** as you can see in the geological feature images below. Toca do Boqueirão means **Boqueirão** lair (or hiding, resting, sleeping place; **refuge**). Toca do Boqueirão da Pedra Furada means essentially the peaceful Boqueirão area of Pedra Furada, basically the subtitle of this novella. Brazil's Serra da Capivara National Park is known for the amazing cave art that fills the place. It's located in a place that's difficult to reach, where bushes grow in abundance, decorated with protective thorns, which may be a reason some of the art is in such great shape. Admittedly some parts of the wall are falling off or crumbling, destroyed by weather and insects. Examples of the fantastic cave art of sites in the Serra da Capivara National Park appear below. Some are from the Boqueirão location. Cave art depicts an active, thriving community in this remote location. Some art seems to portray ritual behavior around a tree.

To see images that follow in color and larger size, go to my blog: www.booksbybonnye.com/blog/

Pedra Furada, Serra da Capivara National Park (Arturo
Warchavchik CCA-SA 3.0)

Serra da Capivara Land Forms (Diego Rego Monteiro, CCA-SA 3.0)

Toca do Boqueirão Cave Art (Diego Rego Monteiro,
CCA-SA 4.0)

Serra da Capivara National Park Cave Art (B4unorocha
CCA-SA 3.0)

Serra da Capivara National Park Cave Art (Artur Warchavchik
CCA-SA 3.0)

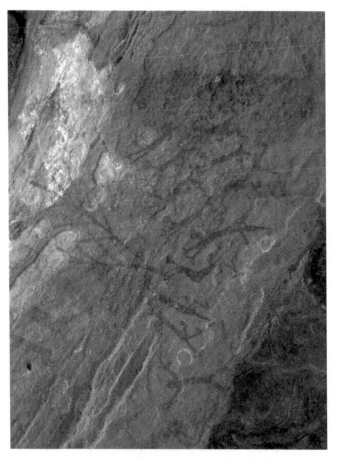

Serra da Capivara National Park—Tree Ritual (Vitor 1234, CCA-SA 3.0)

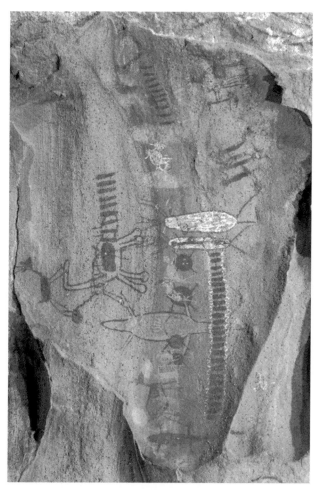

Serra da Capivara National Park (Artur Warchavchik
CCA-SA 3.0)

Serra da Capivara National Park (Augusto Pessoa CCA-SA 3.0)

Note: the white gash at the bottom mid-center of the image is a piece of wall that has fallen off.

Serra da Capivara National Park (Diego Rego Monteiro
CCA-SA 3.0)

Serra da Capivara National Park (Willame carvalho e silva
CCA-SA 3.0)

THE CHARACTERS

Bru

Perru + *Tamin* | Erru + *Gop*

Efum + *Magul*	Latap *Potu*	Gol + *Chim*	Abut + *Mu*
Fig	Lamut	Bid	*Aps*
Tau	*E-ha*	Moa	Due
Maru	*Toha*	*Eko*	*Purl*
Vale	*Femur*	*Mego*	Mat
Emog	Lahan	*Atella*	*Sue*
	Tero	Tupal	*Tab*
	Lig	Kop	Hun
	Newborn	Mug	Ott
			Ang
			Newborn

When the story begins the people live on the sunrise side just off the foot of the Andes Mountains in the west of South America. Years before the story, Manday, Gol, and others explored extensively parts of the land that became Brazil. The story begins with Manday, a man from the Orros tribe, having just warned the people they are under threat from the Molgray, a tribe living about midway down the sunset side of the Andes Mountains. The Chief of the Molgray people is Zuntab. (Note: italics = females.)

Part 1

"We must discover what is happening at Molgray," Latap's voice had become forceful and a bit too high pitched. Perru's face was immobile except for the faint vertical line that formed between his brows. Perru, Latap's father, sat with his legs straight out in front of him. His knees were stiff and painful, so kneeling or sitting cross-legged like other men was impossible.

"That involves extreme risk after what we heard from Manday of the Orros. I enjoin you to be careful," Bru added, knowing it was probably unnecessary. The elder's voice was cracking and people had to listen carefully to hear all the words he spoke.

Erru, Bru's eldest son sat up straighter. "We should send several to talk to Zuntab." He looked at his sons Gol and Abut, concerned.

"I disagree," Efum broke into the discussion quickly, almost rudely. "I will gladly go alone to visit Chief Zuntab, not to endanger anyone else. If it's as bad as we've heard, we cannot spare multiple risks." By risks he meant loss of life. Everyone knew it, even the children.

Magul, Efum's wife showed no emotion, but she already knew Efum would likely go there alone. She feared that if he did, he would not return. She felt a knife stab her chest. She *saw* it. That's how they'll take him, she realized.

In the deep rockshelter that was the home of their Elder, Bru, who was either father, grandfather, or great-grandfather to each, there was great anxiety. They'd heard that the Molgray intended to rule the various groups of peoples and would take over violently, if they didn't agree to his offer of alliance. Zuntab, leader of the Molgray, intended to be the only regional power. There would be no division of power. Every equinox and every solstice, Zuntab would collect tribute from all. Manday of the Orros had brought the news. Manday was a man of integrity, one to be trusted. The Orros were good people.

"I will leave in the morning—alone," Efum said firmly. "If I fail to return in three days, consider I no longer breathe." He was acutely aware of the risk and tried to hide his concern. His son, Fig, marveled at his father's courage.

The fire sputtered and sparks flew all about. A large log fell to the ground. The group was deathly quiet.

Maru watched her father. *He should not go to that dangerous place alone*, she thought. Maru at seven years old was too young to speak out. She would be punished, if she spoke out at council. She held her belly. It hurt. She knew it took one day to reach Molgray and that meant crossing the mountain and descending the other side. It would take as long to return. He would meet with bad people. With jaguars, terror birds, bears, snakes, wolves, and other predators, it was dangerous. She loved her father. She didn't want anything to happen to him. Conflict raged in her tiny body.

"You are our best go-between," Perru, his father admitted. "What gift should you take?" Perru asked.

Maru was horrified. She realized that her father would go alone to Molgray, and nobody would disagree with the decision. She quietly expelled gas, hoping to reduce the pain in her gut.

Abut said, "I suggest he carry a basket of our special mushrooms. This is the only place they grow, and Zuntab is fond of them, or at least he is reported to be fond of them."

"Good idea," Gol added, trying to sound enthusiastic, "They don't weigh much, so the transportation will be easy. They can be ready when you leave. We have many dried."

"Good time of year for that," Latap said.

"All are agreed, then?" Efum asked.

No one spoke. All nodded. Maru wanted to scream. She held the scream in the lowest part of her gut.

The council broke apart and the people went to their homes.

Once inside their small cave, Magul touched Efum's shoulder. "Husband," she said, "This is a dangerous act you plan. What happens if you fail to return?"

Efum turned and hugged her to him warmly. "You will know you were loved with a deep passion," he replied. "You will be helped by each member of our people. You know that. We have the fewest children, so you will be the least burden on the people."

"You're a good man, Efum. I've known that since we were children. I don't want to lose you. I have, however, accepted that this is what you will do. Children, it is time for you to go to your sleeping places." Magul's words came out calmly. As she chose, the feelings of certain loss she hid deep inside were effectively failing to corrupt her spoken words. She was chilled to the innermost tubes of her gut. Concurrently, she felt immense pride for Efum. He was a good man and his concern was for the people. He considered the welfare of the people more than he considered himself. Always.

Quietly the children settled in their places for the night.

When Efum awakened at daybreak, he gathered the weapons he planned to carry. He took his backpack that had been prepared overnight and placed it at the doorway. He picked up the mushrooms that had been put into a new bag, decorated with stitching that looked like mushrooms. Efum hugged and kissed Magul and began to walk toward the path. Hardly on the path, he found he was not alone. His son, Fig, had joined him.

"Go back, Son," he ordered in a quiet but very firm voice.

"Father, you cannot go alone."

"I go alone. If anything happens to me, you must help care for your mother. You slow my progress. Obey me and return home."

While Fig lowered his head in submission, hidden carefully in the woods was Maru. She would stay far enough behind her father, until it was too late for him to send her home. She learned from Fig. At home she had bunched up clothing under her sleeping skins to make it seem she slept. It would be a while before her deviousness would be noticed. Maru brought nothing with her for the trip.

Fig passed her on his way home without even sensing her presence. Already he bore the responsibility for his family.

After he had gone around a turn in the trail, Maru emerged from her hiding place in the forest and began to follow her father, hoping to be quiet enough not to be detected or give him cause to suspect he was being followed.

When Fig arrived back home, he met his uncle Latap on the path.

"I thought I'd find you here," Latap said with a smile. "You're a good son. Now, come help. We're building several rafts. We expect your father to return to warn us to leave quickly. The plan is to follow this big river all the way to the salt water. We'll follow the salt water south to another river, which we will follow north. There is a sanctuary we already have planned to seek. Gol has been there and knows the way." Latap knew his nephew, Fig, was frightened. So was he.

Usually reticent, his words poured out, "Why didn't we just go? Why did my father have to take the risk?"

"It's always wise to verify what's suspected, Fig. Remember that. It is a very big thing to take the voyage we plan to take. People could die along the way. You don't do things like that without much reason."

"I understand," Fig replied, though he sorely wished he were with his father.

About noon, Efum began to hunger, so he pulled a piece of mammoth jerky from his pouch and began to chew on it. He stopped for a moment to drink water and continued his walk. Behind him Maru was having some difficulty keeping up. She had to run or jog often just to keep up with his walking. After drinking, Efum listened carefully to the noises of the forest. Something didn't seem quite right, but he couldn't decide what it was. He resumed his trek.

The forest was darkening, for the sun was below the mountaintops. Efum reached the top and sat down to view the area below. The village of Molgray wasn't terribly far. He should be there before dark. On the sun-setting side of the mountain, dark came later. Then, Efum heard the noise that had been intruding on his thoughts all day. He was furious and frightened.

"Come here!" he demanded, and Maru slipped out of the woods and showed herself, still breathing hard.

Efum thought it was Fig until he saw Maru. Something in him broke. She loved too strongly for someone so young, he thought.

"Why are you here?" he demanded in a hoarse whisper, already knowing the answer.

"I must know you are safe," came the reply timidly.

"Under almost any other circumstances, I'd beat you with a stick until you bled," he said through clenched teeth. "Now, I have to look out for both of us. I am terribly disappointed in you right now." His voice was quiet and severe. Far away. So very different. Maru had never seen this side of her father.

"Come, have some jerky," he said. She came and took the piece he handed her. She sat silently and ate the jerky. She had been hungry for a long time that day.

"I will tell you how it will be. Disobey me and you may die. Do you understand? This adventure of yours is not for children."

"Yes, Father," she replied completely contrite.

"Outside Molgray there is a great tree. The spirit of the tree is protection. From the tree you will be able to see what happens when I go to the place. If the worst happens and they kill me, you must stay in the tree well hidden and silent until night. Do not expose yourself. The tree will protect you. When it's fully dark, you must come down from the tree, as long as you are sure no one is nearby. You must follow the trail we took to arrive here. There is a full moon so you can see. You must maintain silence no matter what happens. If you have to cry, wait until you return home. At home you must warn the people to leave immediately. Maru, promise me you will do as I ask. Otherwise, I must turn around and take you home."

"Father, I will not disappoint you again. I will do exactly what you say. I promise." Maru was still glad she had followed her father, but she ached to have disappointed him so much.

They finished the jerky. Her father put the bag of jerky around her neck so she had all of it. He led her on the path to Molgray. After cresting the mountain and descending to the top of a hill on the west side, they reached the tree he'd mentioned. Maru was astonished at the size of the tree. It was a great tree, full of leaves and many exceptionally long branches. She'd never seen a tree that covered so much space. Efum climbed the tree and told her to follow him. She did. He showed her where to sit to be out of easy observation from the path, and yet she could see the village below.

"Remember what I told you. If they kill me, stay silent. Wait until dark to leave and be sure no people are nearby. Go home trying to leave as few prints on the dirt as possible. If they kill me you must warn our people. That's what you must do, since you followed me. You cannot let all our people die."

"I obey, my Father. You think they will kill you?" she asked in a whisper with her face down. Horror pierced her.

"I am almost certain."

"Oh, Father!" she whispered with a sob, reaching out for a hug. For the first time the sense of the size of the risk struck her. She realized that she might very well have to return home alone. He hugged her—tight.

Efum held her to him for a long time. "Silence now," he said and went back down the tree. She watched the route he took down the tree. One way or another, she'd have to descend, and she needed to know how. For the present she watched him as he left. He went to the east from where they came and then turned north, walking carefully so as not to disturb vegetation, for there was no path where he walked. Then he came down a different pathway, avoiding the one he could have taken from the tree. Maru watched as he approached the village below from the north. She realized he'd been as devious as she had been that morning, making it appear she slept when she was gone. He'd made it appear he came from a path that did not lead to her home. She watched, eager for his return.

She saw two men stop her father as he reached the edge of the path to the village. They walked on either side of him, leading him to a man with a bear head and skin covering him. She thought the man must be very hot inside all that furred skin. The man with the bear skin took the mushrooms and laid them beside a hut. The men sat near a small hearth to talk.

Maru watched as the four men talked. Her father laughed at something. He laughed loud enough that she could hear him. She felt relieved. All the men laughed. She saw one of them rise instantly while they laughed, and, in a fast swipe, the man stabbed her father, causing blood to spurt straight out from his chest. She covered her mouth with both hands to stifle a building scream. She knew he was dead. She had no word for treachery in her vocabulary. Word or not, treachery grew instant horror in the pit of her soul. Then to increase the horror, while tears fell from her eyes silently, the two men cut off her father's head. She gawked, disbelieving, as they carried the head to a pole and shoved it onto the pole so it looked out at her. She was absolutely terrified, didn't want to look, couldn't fully take in what her eyes saw, but could not pull her gaze away. Her father's head stared at her from a pole!

Maru was stricken with both disbelief and horror. Her mind was empty of words. She wanted to climb down the tree and flee immediately to her home. Her father's face stared at her. His eyes were still open. She did what he'd told her to do. She remained in the tree waiting for dark, wondering when the sun would finally set. Seeing the dead face of her father staring back at her, she felt utterly alone, somehow not herself, frightened beyond any fear she'd ever experienced, totally lacking in courage. She heard a noise and saw two men, the two who killed her father, walk up the path where her father entered the slope down to the village. They were looking to see whether he'd been accompanied. Maru understood. She didn't move or make a sound. The men returned to the village and began to walk up the path that led to the tree where she perched.

Maru trembled. Her hand's grip slipped on the branch and her chest fell to the limb near the trunk where she sat. The branch she had been gripping slashed her forearm so it bled. Maru hardly noticed. Her awareness was that her action caused the limb to shake all the way to the end. Her horror intensified. Maru froze in place from fear of discovery. She didn't want her head on a pole. She had to warn her people. The men squinted at the tree briefly, seeing nothing. One of them said, "Accursed monkeys!" and they laughed fake laughs. The men, finding no tracks at all, returned to the village never actually reaching the tree where Maru hid.

While the sun made its slow move to the horizon, Maru, still with a mind devoid of words, touched a mimosa leaf with her forefinger. The little leaflets closed. It drew her attention and the image burned itself into her mind. She touched another leaf and the same thing happened. And then awash again in her horror, she looked at her father's head on the pole.

Finally, darkness came. In the village the men began to beat drums and sing. They made enough noise for her to feel safe enough to descend and begin the return home to warn her people.

The need to save her people helped Maru function despite her stark terror. Part of her was doing what had to be done, while the other part was closed off, as if wrapped in semi-soft leather, and put out of sight in the back of a cave. She held onto the idea of living people, people she must protect. She tried to push her horror far away and banish the vision of her father's head on a pole.

Maru didn't think of the risks of being alone in the forest at night then. She didn't consider the predators that lurked at night. Her one horror was the men below on the other side of the mountain. She had a single goal: reach home to warn her people. Her father had been right. The moon made the path visible at night. She wasted no time and ran as fast as she could until her breathing was, she was sure, too loud. Loud enough to attract predators. She cupped her hand over her mouth. She walked listening intently to the night noise, trying to think only of living people.

Maru didn't know where the halfway point was, but she knew it must be after leaving the slope of the mountain. She reached the flat land exhausted, tears still falling, fear beginning to creep in as she jumped over a large snake on the path that had something not much smaller than she in its gut. She knew the snake couldn't bother her because the huge body it contained permitted nothing but digestion, so at some distance from it, she sat and tried to gather her wits about her. She shook and permitted herself to cry with a little noise. Then, she realized she needed to move hastily to warn her people. Terror gripped her soul, but she had to warn them. She could not let what happened to her father happen to her people. She must not. For a moment she envisioned heads of all the people on poles. Horror quickened her pace. She shivered but not from night chill. This came from within her. She was responsible for the people. She kept repeating the words to herself.

After a while she slowed, the fast pace beginning to hurt her chest more than she could bear. Maru briefly wondered what she'd do if she reached home and the heads of all the people were on poles. Quickly, she changed thoughts to those living and ran again, but this time, it was just a constant jog. She wanted to reach home faster than it took to reach the protection tree. A tree fell in the forest.

Maru jumped. She had no idea why it fell, but she continued her jog, speeding up a little. A breeze sprang up from the east, and it cooled her down. Finally, in the east the sun was beginning to rise. She took heart. Color returned to the tree tops and finally the ground. She smelled home before she saw it. She raced into the tiny village and ran right into her uncle, Latap.

"Now, we know you live. What happened?"

Maru shook all over, still terrified. She slowed her breathing before trying to reply. Finally, she said, "My father's head's on a pole at Molgray." She wept, no longer crushing but rather releasing the sounds of sobbing. Her shaking resumed.

It took a moment before Latap's mind received the full impact of the message. His brother was dead. He called the alarm, "Council! Council! Council!" His voice carried well into the forest. He took Maru by her wrist and headed to Bru's cave.

"We have no time to spare," he said once all were assembled. "Maru, tell them what you told me."

Maru looked at the assembly. She was to speak at council? Slowly she found the words between the sobs, "My father's head—on pole—at Molgray." The words shot from her mouth as she saw again in her mind the dreadful scene in memory. The horror of the words stunned the people. To be dead was one thing. To have one's head on a pole—that was quite another. Who could have ever imagined such a thing?

Each one of the people was horrified. They immediately activated the plan for departure. No one took the time to think what the experience must have been for Maru.

Magul did not make a sound, for she had been as prepared as possible. That Maru returned alone told her all she needed to know. She simply had let tears fall from her eyes, as her expectation became real to her. Magul could not hold back the tears. They fell as waterfalls after a great rain but in silence. She felt as if something inside her died to join her husband, but she had to revive it. She had children to raise. Magul understood that Maru felt obliged to follow her father. It was no surprise when she lifted the sleeping skin and found a pile of clothing. She realized that had she been Maru, she'd have done the same thing. She noticed Maru was shaking seemingly unable to control herself. She motioned for her daughter to join her. Maru came and Magul held her tight to her chest. Magul unfastened the bag of jerky from around Maru's neck and removed it. In time the girl calmed a little. Neither spoke.

"It is day," Erru said with great volume, "We must go now. Let us make the most of the time we have."

The people had already prepared the rafts. They were set to leave and the rafts were well provisioned. They had four rafts. There were now forty-three people, since Efum was gone. There were at least three men age fifteen or more for each raft, not counting Bru, who was eighty years old, and women were as able as men to pole a raft. That provided nine more people to guide the rafts. They would travel through the day and night.

All went to the river and stood near the raft they were to take. Erru numbered the people, and as soon as all were accounted for, they boarded the rafts and began their travel to the sea. It would not take long to reach the wide river, and once there, they would feel some sense of safety. No other rafts were in the area. If the Molgray followed, it would take a full day to build one that could be trusted.

Gol had prepared the people that they would remain on the raft until they reached the sea except to hunt, and then only hunters would leave the rafts. The shores were homes for jaguars, crocodiles, great snakes, poisonous spiders, and biting insects. Shore provided no safety at all. Instead shore time could cause casualties and slow their progress, if men from Molgray pursued them. What Gol didn't tell the people initially was that they'd be on the rafts for about half a year. Gol's prior knowledge came from the time he had taken the journey with Manday and others from the nearby village to explore their great land.

The men had prepared both poles to push the rafts along and oars for use when in deeper water with current. Their rafts had a rudder in the rear. Men had used rafts for brief fishing trips, so they were not unaccustomed to handling the watercraft. They had no real experience with the deep, fast river. It would widen significantly. Gol tried to prepare them. Gol was grateful that they went with the current instead of against it. He'd done both. Going with the current took no great strength.

Once they were moving on the water, Latap came to Magul's side and seated himself. "You know that all of us grieve with you?"

Magul nodded.

"We will all stand beside you to provide any help you need. You will never be alone."

"Thank you, Latap," Magul replied slightly distracted, as she had temporarily retreated to a part of her soul reserved only for thoughts of Efum—a part of her soul where pain was fierce, yet she was still able to function. Emog, her two-year-old son stirred in her lap. She prepared to feed him.

They were in the slow, shallow waters of their homeland and poling was required. Four people at each raft were poling. Gol was on the first raft, and he led the people through the water. Palm trees and shrubs hung over the water and the day, though off to a horrifying beginning, was a beautiful one with blue sky and few clouds.

Children were fascinated with the rafts and the change in their lives. They sat where they had been assigned to sit and talked very quietly among themselves. There were few young children. A great sickness had run through the people some years ago and many of the very young had died of fevers. On the raft Magul had a two-year-old; Potu, Latap's wife, had a newborn; Chim, Gol's wife, had a three- and one-year-old; and Mu, Abut's wife, had a three-year-old and a newborn. Magul and Potu each also had a five-year-old; Chim and Mu had six-year-old children. The people treasured children. Those who had survived the sickness were not viewed as children despite their age, because they were more mature from their experience. The sickness had lasted a long time. Some parents realized sadly that the bodies of their children remained behind, no longer to sleep near their people. Their consolation was that they lay among many of their own, not abandoned alone in the wilderness.

As they had been instructed to do, mothers warned children again of the dangers of being near the edges of the rafts. No mother wanted to lose one. The children were told not to cause trouble—to obey. They were a people without a rebellious spirit. Children were obedient, except in the case of Maru or Fig, both of whom were forgiven for the love they had for their father.

Maru was at the back of the third raft. She lay there looking up at the trees that overhung the water. She couldn't see the trees for the images that haunted her mind and the tears that clouded her vision. She'd try to fix her attention on the trees above, when a vision of blood spurting from her father's chest would crush her, or memory of his head on a pole would frighten her witless. Maru wanted to run from the images but didn't know how. She missed her father's warmth, his presence, and his smile. She ached that the last he knew of her, he expressed such disappointment. She had hurt Efum just before he died. There was no way to make it right. She ached and could find no cure.

She saw Latap stand up from her mother's side. Her mother laid Emog beside her. He had been fed and he was sleepy. Her five-year-old brother Vale was talking to Latap's seven-year-old son, Tero. Both watched the shore and talked about what they saw there. Maru tried to listen to their chatter, but she could not make the sound of the drums and singing at Molgray leave her thoughts. She continued to relive the run and chest pain of her retreat home and let silent tears fall from her eyes again. She was overwhelmed. Mercifully, she fell to sleep.

The day constantly turned to days and more days and more days. They divided up the poling and rowing so that they traveled during the day and at night. The river trip became a way of life. Occasionally, they'd see an open place. If hunters noticed food animals, they'd pull the rafts to the shore, leave all on the rafts except a few hunters, and quickly attend to the hunt. The youngest men would scour the banks for wood for the hearths and mosses for the women while the men hunted.

When hunters were successful, animals were brought to the rafts and bled and butchered as they traveled. Gourd scoops of water cleaned the mess away. They thought it safer than trying to bleed and butcher on land. They knew nothing about the ways of this land. They cooked meat, small pieces at a time over a large flat stone provided for each raft as a base for the hearth. Women fed each as the meat cooked. Hearths on the rafts were smaller than those on land that could cook more at a time. Fish supplied additional food as did water plants from the river that could be pulled up as they traveled along. It wasn't a comfortable trip, but it worked.

Fear of the Molgray and the terror regarding what those westerners might do spurred them on.

Maru was struggling. She had stopped talking. Magul tried to help her, realizing she continued to relive the time with gruesome images stored in her memory. She was desperate to help Maru but just didn't know how. Latap observed the dilemma, and he tried to help.

"Talk to me, Maru," he said gently one evening, seating himself beside her. "What haunts you?"

Maru did not respond, so Latap picked her up and held her. "Maru, you must speak to me. It is required," he said with gentle force.

Maru squirmed wishing to disappear.

"Maru, it's time. You are required to speak to me. What haunts you?"

"I keep seeing it. I cannot stop remembering." The words slid out as water would slide from her hands.

"Tell me what you see," he probed.

"No!" she said defiantly.

"Why not?" he asked.

"I'll see it again," she replied with dismay.

"You'll see it anyway, won't you?"

"Yes," she said very quietly, shutting her eyes as if that could make the images stop.

"Maru, the things you see won't stop by trying to push them away. There's more to it. What really bothers you?"

"My father's dead."

"What else?" he asked gently.

"I disappointed him," she sobbed, pulling her knees to her chest and holding them there. "He was terribly, fiercely angry with me. I couldn't make it right. He died. I couldn't make it right."

Maru wept in the pit of heartbreak. Latap was amazed a child that age could feel that deeply. He held her to him, trying the best he could to comfort her, and then an idea struck him.

"Maru, why was your father angry with you?"

"I disobeyed. I was there causing him to have to look after me as well as himself."

"There's more to it," he assured her.

"What?" she asked.

"In that moment, your father knew how much you loved him. He recognized your love for him was full. He knew you had traveled hidden, until it was too late for him to send you back. Men like to have plans go the way they set them. You prevented his plan from going the way he wanted. He was angry because he loved you, not because he was disappointed and had to care for you. He didn't want you to die on the trip, and he was almost certain he would die. He wanted you to live because he loved you. He knew you had to be extremely strong to do what you would have to do alone. He feared you might die."

"What?" she asked. Maru couldn't seem to entertain any idea in conflict with disappointing her father. Here Latap was telling her he died knowing how much she loved him, not how disappointed he was with her. It didn't fit her thoughts.

"Are you a man? A father?" Latap asked her louder, almost demanding.

"Of course not," Maru replied, indignant, letting go of her legs and sitting up straight.

"You think you know how a man thinks, how a father thinks?" he asked.

Maru looked at her uncle. She replied, "No."

Latap moved her to sit beside him and put his arm around her. "Well, I do. Your father would have seen you there; aware you were near great danger. He knew you knew of only the smallest of the risks. He knew your courage was displayed because you loved him. You were willing to walk into danger with him. That kind of love is amazing. He had to show displeasure because you were disobedient, but he was warmed to his seventh soul, knowing the extent of your love for him. He feared you might not make it back home alive. He had to do everything he could do to help you make it home. He knew without him you might fear. He had to make you feel responsible. Responsible for your people. It is the way of fathers to feel responsible—your father especially. He was always responsible. He knew responsibility would give you the courage to make it home to warn us."

"I was not courageous coming home; I was terrified," she admitted.

Latap brushed her hair from her forehead and away from her eyes. He dried her tears. "Courage is not separate from fear—but despite fear. Fear can grow courage or paralysis, like an animal that fails to move. Your father feared going to Molgray, but he did it for the people—to be certain of the need to flee—he did it despite his fear. That is courage."

Maru was overwhelmed. She'd heard a different way of understanding the effects of fear. A father's way of seeing. *Her* father's way of seeing? He wasn't disappointed because she couldn't make things right?

"Then, there was a way I could make things right?" she asked.

"Yes, Maru, and you did it. You made it home and warned us. We left before they could arrive to stop us. Despite your fear, you came home quickly through the forest to save your people. Your courage saved us. Do you not understand that? Make it right? That more than made it right!"

"But my father never knew."

"Your father knew. He knew when he made you feel responsible for your people. He knew then you'd do your very best to make it home to warn us. He hoped you wouldn't lose courage in the forest, becoming prey to some predator. Instead, responsibility for the people would help you show courage. That would make predators less likely to attack. Your willingness to warn us more than made it right, Maru. If that's what's bothering you, you're a silly child. You've made up a burden to carry that isn't yours. Put the burden down. Put it down, now."

Maru didn't move. She carefully considered what Latap was saying. She went through in her mind the last moments of her father's life. She tried to see what Latap said. Did it fit what she saw? She realized with growing acceptance that it did fit. Her father would have been surprised to find her there near Molgray. He would have known she knew about the risks. He would have known she loved him enough to take the same risks. She didn't leave him completely disappointed in her. He also recognized her love. And he made it right by giving her the reason to make it home alive—their love of the people. She went through the last moments over and over. She could follow Latap's interpretation. It did fit, and no, she didn't think like a man. A father. She thought like a child.

Maru looked up at Latap. "I think I understand, Uncle," she said quietly.

"Now, Maru, I want you to understand that you've been looking backwards too long. You must change to a forward-looking girl now. What happened is past. Life goes on. You have learned two things, and you must not forget. You learned that your father was actually proud of you for what you did and would do. He knew you loved him enough to share his risk. The other thing you learned is that even when things are tough, you must go through life looking forward, not backward. You had to look forward so you could save your people. You did that. You remained in the tree not moving to do what had to be done. Your action saved us a whole day to avoid the people from Molgray. Then, you started looking backwards. You came up with an idea that you failed your father and gave him terrible thoughts just before he died. That was a creation of your mind, not reality. That wrong idea could have destroyed your life now and for the future. Have you learned?"

"I think so, Uncle," Maru replied with some recovered feeling. Gazing upward at the trees, she thought the green was somehow greener, the blue of the sky a little bluer. She saw a black-and-white capuchin monkey in the tree directly overhead. It was silent, eating something, watching. Maru saw the yellow flowers at the top of the Brazil-nut tree, and it made her salivate. It would be a while before the nuts fell to the ground, exploding the cases to reveal the tasty, hard nuts. She saw some things other than terrible scenes endlessly repeating.

Latap helped her up and she returned to her place on the raft. Latap looked at Magul. She smiled at him a sweet smile. She'd heard. She understood that he'd given a gift to Maru, the gift of absolution. Magul was grateful. Latap felt drained but pleased with himself.

A shout from the second raft rang through the area. Pointing to the north shore, the people saw a herd of camels. Carefully they poled the rafts to the clearing. They were delighted at the thought of having camel to eat. They'd been days without what they considered real meat.

Hunters led by Abut came at the camels from the woodland. They killed four. Each raft had a camel to bleed, butcher, and eat. As they began their drift once more, the people looked forward to this unexpected treat.

They continued their drift eastward. Early one morning, the first raft sounded an alert. There were people on the southern shore. Unless the shore people swam out, they were too far away to spear the rafts. Neither group was prepared to see other people. The ones on shore gawked. They did not appear war-like, but Gol had been carefully taught not to trust the shore people, and he steered more to the north, insisting on avoidance. Part of the fascination was that the skin color of the people on shore was very dark brown, where the skin color of the people on the rafts was light tan. The shore dwellers had hair that held together, rather than straight and flowing as theirs was. The shore dwellers appeared to have teeth so white they glowed. They wore skirts of grasses not skins as the people did. The people on both sides waved to each other and smiled, but the rafts did not slow or stop. The men simply became more cautious, unsure what they'd find on the shores, quite amazed to find people living along the river. They would be more vigilant in scanning the shores.

As the group traveled they taught the younger ones from age eleven and older how to pole and row. They taught them to steer to avoid objects in the river. They taught them how to check the ropes that held the raft logs together and how to pull the rafts to land for hunters to gather food.

Maru sat beside her mother one hot, humid afternoon. She noticed that Aug, Abut and Mu's little three-year-old daughter, was missing.

"Where's Aug?" Maru asked, not at all certain she wanted to know.

Magul considered how to say it. "One evening she dangled her feet in the water. A crocodile took her." She watched Maru to see what effect the words might have on her.

Maru covered her eyes. The vision of her father's head flashed through her mind. Magul had suspected she might set off the images her daughter still experienced, but she would not withhold truth.

"Where was I?" Maru asked very quietly.

"You slept from the scenes you remembered. You could not have saved her, Maru."

"That's true, but I feel that somehow I might have."

"Put it out of your mind, Maru. Do not look for trouble where it doesn't exist." Magul put her arm around Maru's shoulders.

About two thirds of the way into the voyage, the rains came. It rained a lot, swelling the river and increasing the speed of the current. At some times the rain was so heavy and the current so swift that the men tied the rafts together so that no one would become separated from the group. In desperation they parked the rafts at the shore and cut down some poles and gathered huge flexible leaves. They built shelters on the rafts. It was a good idea and the people regained a lot of comfort. Keeping fires going was much easier.

As they continued voyaging the closeness brought some of the young together so constantly that bonds formed. Bid, the son of Gol, took Aps, daughter of Abut, as his wife; Lamut, Latop's eldest son, took Purl, Abut's daughter, for his wife; Due, Abut's son, took E-ha, Latop's daughter, as his wife. Before they reached the salt water, Aps, Purl, and E-ha would all be pregnant. Magul carried the child Efum gave her the night before he left for Molgray.

The people hungered. It had been days since they'd found food animals.

"What in all the Creator's imagining is that?" Fig shouted from the third raft.

He was pointing to the southern shore. At first no one saw what he saw, so well camouflaged was it. Then the creature moved and they saw it. A huge crocodile, a giant one compared to what they'd previously seen. It was dark in color, resting on the riverbank against wet soil, where it blended in perfectly.

"That crocodile must be the size of three maybe four men from its head to tail's end!" Gol exclaimed, as he identified for the others what the animal was.

"Can we eat them?" Abut asked.

"Yes, but that one's too large for us. We need to search the banks for some of smaller size," Gol said.

The people watched the huge beast as they drifted by. It was formidable.

"Look over there!" Gol pointed to the other side of the river. "That's what they look like when in the water. You hardly see them. These big ones look like logs. They go off with careless men before anyone can stop them." Gol warned the children again to stay in the center of the rafts.

By evening the people again had seen no food animals. The night's chill was upon them. They had no success fishing. They shared the greens they'd pulled from the river and tried to fool themselves into feeling full.

"On the bank over there!" Mego, Gol's twelve-year-old daughter shouted, pointing, "There are some crocodiles that are a lot smaller."

The four rafts pulled over well beyond the crocodiles. The hunters followed the example Gol set.

They tied cordage to their large spears. Six men left the rafts and headed through the brush on the riverbank. They approached the animals from the land side. Snout to tail they were about the length a man was tall. They hurled their spears at the crocodiles and speared six of them. The animals headed for the water while men held onto the cordage so they couldn't escape. Some crocodiles rolled trying to dislodge the spears. Bid and Due took their clubs and, carefully avoiding the jaws and tails of the animals, they quickly clubbed the crocodiles in the heads. Two of the crocodiles escaped, but the men had managed to kill one for each raft. Quickly they carried their prey to the rafts and began the process of turning the creatures to food. Children came over when the crocodiles were loaded on the rafts to touch the skin and examine the animals closely. It was late into the night by the time they had food, but they ate under the massive array of stars above, grateful for the abundance of food which satisfied their hunger. The meat tasted far better than they expected, considering the appearance of the beasts.

The people would travel the river for a long time. They saw very few food animals along the way, except crocodiles. They credited the life-saving nourishment from the crocodiles as a gift from their Creator to keep them on their way to their refuge. Crocodiles lived in abundance along the shores. From that time the people never hungered again.

One night they drifted along a slow moving part of the river where it was very wide. Perru decided to tell the New Land Story. All listened, finding comfort in the words repeated exactly as they had been for uncountable years. It told of the extraordinary migration of their people across the Pacific Ocean to South America, but they had no concept of how significant their story was.

"We left our land of desolation. There had been wars and famine. The land became as dust. It was a bad time. The Creator told us through the Sacred Land Spirit that we must leave. We made great rafts. We knew the way of the sea, but we had never taken such a distant voyage. We traveled from the land where the sun sets to the land where the sun rises. We traveled for a very long time, using the flow of the great sea to help us. We ate what the sea provided and captured water in the night's provision of dewfall and rain on skins we stretched out."

We lost people as we traveled. Along the way we met Great Sea Spirits. They had kind eyes and great arms that hit the water. They used tails to hit the water also. They sang songs to us in moans that struck us so that we vibrated with the moans. Finally, we arrived at New Land. The land was endless. Instead of desolation as our land had been, this one was filled with great green plants. Food animals roamed the land everywhere, unafraid of us. There were animals the likes of which we'd never seen. We rejoiced. In time we found that the Creator wanted us to move on. Great shaking of the land brought tall waters towards us, carrying some people to the sea. We left for the other side of the mountains to be safe from the tall waters. The mountains made barriers of protection for us from the risks of the sea. There we found a place to live where food was plentiful and our people were healthy and happy. That New Land is what we just left behind." Perru added, "We now travel by raft as we did in the far past. We travel to a different part of this New Land to a refuge from warring people. This New Land will protect our people. It will be good. Until the Creator chooses for us to move, we will thrive in this new part of the New Land."

It was a story of hope. The people hadn't heard the story for quite some time. It energized them to travel on, knowing that they were going to a better place. Each day brought them closer.

Maru noticed a kapok tree with a thick base where the roots began way above the ground and seemed to glide groundward in a curve. Maru and other children used to climb the sloping root structures to the trunk of kapok trees. They tried to run up the roots, but usually had to use their hands before reaching the tree trunk. She had to be careful not to fall and sprain an ankle, which happened once. A feeling of emptiness passed over her, when she thought of home. She tried to look to the future. It was hard.

Maru listened. She remembered the words of her father, when he told her the spirit of the tree was protection. She thought of how that must be. Did the spirit just take on the shape of the tree, or did it grow that way? Was it just that type of tree that was protection or were all trees filled with spirits of protection? Did a spirit just attach itself to that tree? Did it die when the tree died? Or, she wondered, did her father mean the tree was designed for protection, not directly tied to a spirit? Yes, she reasoned, she thought in the manner of a child. There was so much she didn't understand. She relaxed as she mused over the stories of protection that ran through their history. The world was sometimes a place of terror. Maru was sure she knew as much about terror as adults did. Children, she assumed, at least the ones she knew, had no idea of the reality of terror. Their Creator had made spirits of protection along the ways in life, showing a love and providence for the people he made. She marveled at the love the Creator's protection showed her. A tiny bit of doubt about Creators and protection entered her mind, and she firmly pushed it away.

After the story, those who were not rowing found places to stretch out to sleep. The sky above was alive with traveling stars. Some of the people went to sleep immediately while others lay there watching the silent sky above where stars were busily traveling in the darkness. Maru watched. It was a fitting end to the story that night.

Part 2

The people reached the place where the river emptied into the salt water. It was noisy. The salt water was calm, so they expected that is how it would always be. Gol explained the sea could become very rough with large crashing waves pounding the shore. He reminded them that when their people came to New Land, they had to move across the mountains to keep a barrier between themselves and the risks of the sea. During stormy times, they'd have to bring the rafts to shore. For days, however, they rowed southward, just off shore. The sandy beaches were alluring and time off the boat was something all enjoyed. They had bagged a lot of fresh water at Gol's insistence before the water became salty in the river. It had to last until they found another river.

Some of the men took a hunting expedition inland to provide meat. They managed to find some deer, and brought back enough to have a feast. The gentle breeze from the sea kept biting bugs away while they had a great fire to cook the deer meat.

Women had stored cashews, mangoes, avacadoes, jicama. They found some collard greens, yams, and Brazilian spinach to add to the feast.

Standing in the water to push rafts to shore, a big fish bit Amut on the leg. It was painful but healed well.

Magul had to continue to chase Emog, who wanted to step into the surf. He was unafraid of the water and too young to understand the reason he was told to stay back from the water's edge. She realized she simply had to make him obey. Latap noticed the boy's interest in the water. He took Emog and walked to the water with him. He took Emog where the water was over his head and let him go. At first Emog enjoyed the water but quickly he needed to breathe. Latap permitted him to struggle in the surf and then he pulled him up. The little one coughed and spit up water. Magul was beside herself with worry. Finally, Latap brought the terrified two-year-old back to Magul.

"Let me know if that doesn't keep him away from the water," Latap told her.

Fortunately, that took care of the little one's interest in the sea. He stayed close to Magul in awe of his uncle, afraid of the sea.

Great fortune followed their voyage around the land's curve from the north to the south and then westward. The sea remained calm the whole time. They found the river that flowed from the north and began to row upriver. They would have a long voyage and then would have to travel by land to reach their new place in this New Land. There was little hunger on the voyage north. Small crocodiles were available along the shores. There was food, if not in great variety.

At the end of the long voyage, the people disembarked. They remained in the area of disembarkation for ten days. A few of the people experienced the disorientation that comes from sea travel where one feels a shakiness, as if the land moves like the sea. This passed, and they became land creatures again during their brief stay.

While they waited, Abut, Bid, Lamut, Due, Moa, and Fig left for a hunt.

"What on this green earth is that?" Moa, Gol's son, said quietly to the others while pointing to something on a grassy land to the north.

"It looks like an armadillo," Abut replied in a whisper, "but it's huge. Its back has to be as high off the ground as the top of my head! Well, maybe not that high."

"Can we eat it?" Fig whispered.

"I don't see why not. It probably tastes like huge armadillo," Abut replied in his hushed voice with a smile.

Connecting the idea of huge with the sense of taste, as if there were a taste for huge, struck the hunters as humorous at a time when quiet was necessary. They stifled laughter.

"I think we should concentrate on the area between the head and shoulders," Bid said, still amused at huge having a taste. "There doesn't appear to be anyplace else where they're vulnerable, unless it's the belly. I wish my father could see this now."

"Gol probably has already seen them," Due said quietly, since Gol is the one who'd been to this area.

"I keep forgetting that," Bid said laughing in a whisper, which he found hard to do.

The men began to stalk the animals. At a nod from Abut, they rushed the enormous armadillos and speared them at the neck. Their effort was rewarded. The animals had no fear whatsoever of the humans who came at them so quickly.

The hunters returned to the camp with the two giant armadillos. They had bled and gutted the creatures. The hunters butchered one and carried the other animal whole so that the people could see what they looked like. They marveled at the strange creature. Children came up to touch the animals, so they'd know what they felt like. The women eventually received the butchered parts of the animals, and Mu, Abut's wife, and Tamin, Perru's wife, spent the day turning the meat over spits at the fire, preparing for a feast. As the day passed and the women could taste the cooked meat, their delight was that the meat tasted a lot like peccary, a food they enjoyed very much.

At dinner the hunters of the huge armadillos laughed among themselves as they tasted "huge armadillo." They tried to explain the reason for the laughter, but the group looked at them bewildered, not understanding.

Due said, "You probably had to be there to know why it's making us laugh."

A few days later Tupal walked on a hillside just above the campsite. He began to scream. Gol, his father, ran up the hill followed by his brother, Bid. While holding his leg, Tupal pointed to where the snake went. Blood escaped from two holes in the boy's leg. Bid discovered a brown, tan, gray blotched snake with some white on it. He despaired to see the snake's triangular head. Angered, he pursued the snake and using his spearhead, he killed the snake. As the day wore on, Tupal ran fevers and shook. A day later the snake venom took the young boy's life. Tupal had just turned seven, and he was a special friend of Maru. She was devastated.

Their strength returning, the people began the final part of their journey, the trek to their new homes. They carried the body of Tupal so he could sleep among his people. They had to climb through mountains to reach their new land. Having been on the rafts for so long, the people enjoyed the challenges of the mountains, not to mention the variety of food available. The crocodiles had provided food for them, when they would otherwise have starved, but they were tired of crocodile meat.

For three days, out in the open, the people faced a raging storm. They struggled to put up lean-to shelters in the forest. The rain came in downpours. Little children wanted to play in the puddles outside the lean-tos but their mothers pulled them back into the shelters. Finally, the rain left in a windstorm. The sky was clear blue, cloudless following the wind, but a breeze persisted. They traveled onward to their new home.

One evening as they were eating meat from a small sloth, Gol told them that they'd see their new home the next day. The news came as a great shock to all. The most grateful of the people was Bru. He knew when they first reached the sea that he was beginning to fail. He experienced strange heartbeats, and often he was dizzy. He gave all his effort to making it to the new home, because he didn't want to sleep in death far from his people. After the last voyage where they'd rowed upriver, Lamut and Due had carried him on a litter where at first he sat, but for the last few days, he'd lain down while the young men transported him. There was a time when that would have been embarrassing to Bru, but no longer. Having heard that they'd be at the new place the next day, Bru had a triumphal moment. He knew he'd see his people start anew. He would sleep in the care and remembrance of his people.

It was hard for all to sleep that night. The full moon shone down and the stars were out in spectacular profusion. Many wondered how the new place would look. They had seen such variety of land that they had no assurance what they'd find at the end of the trek Gol had led. Finally, the last of the people succumbed and sleep came.

The people awakened to another beautiful day. They gathered their belongings, few as they were, and they sat to eat some food before resuming the trek. At last they began. The people went through a pass in the mountains and saw some strange geologic formations. The rocks looked striped, and Gol explained that they were looking at land that had once been underwater. They knew this rock was softer than some others. It didn't serve well for making spearheads. It did serve well for shelters, and the soft rock could be carved back for more space when necessary. The people continued on, passing places that looked satisfactory for lodging. They went a bit farther and saw, looming above them, a rock with a hole in it, Pedra Furada. They stood staring in awe. It would become the symbol of their homeland.

At a little distance they found the place Gol had been drawn to as a place for them to live. It had some caves in proximity, so they'd have some privacy, but be close enough together, if needed for defense. They called it Boqueirão. The place in time became known as Toca do Boqueirão da Pedra Furado, the peaceful Boqueirão at Pedra Furada.

The people settled upon four main living caves. In the largest, Bru and his son, Perru, with his wife, Tamin, would live with Magul and her children. In the next largest cave, Abut and his wife, Mu, would live with their children. In another cave, Erru and his wife, Gop, would live with Gol and his wife, Chim, and their children. In the last cave, Latap and his wife, Potu, would live with their children. The young people who joined together during the voyage could choose which cave to join as long as no cave was overburdened. The caves weren't deep. There was no great concern; for weather in the area did not often become cold enough to need deep cave protection. A few caves gave the impression that people had lived there a long time ago. There was a hint of hearths and a few pieces of flaked stone.

To tend to the burial of Tupal, Gol, Bid, and Moa quickly dug his grave and buried him. There was tacit relief at the reduction of death odor. It concerned them less than the loss of Tupal, but it had been a constant reminder.

There was a busy time of gathering things to be placed in the caves while a number of the men left for a hunt. Maru walked nearer to Pedra Furada and suddenly she began to weep. Latap noticed her and went to her.

"What is it, Maru? What causes your eyes to leak?"

She pointed to a tree.

Latap was confused. "Your eyes leak because of a tree?"

"There are so few of these. It is the type of tree where I hid."

"What do you mean?"

"When I followed my father to Molgray, he stopped me and made me hide in a tree. He told me words I still find strange. He said I had to hide in that tree, and he told me, 'the spirit of the tree is protection.' I followed him up the tree, and he showed me where to stay. It was a huge tree with limbs that went outstretched for a long distance. There were many leaves. It was this type of tree. This one is just a baby tree."

"Does it make you sad?" Latap asked, as he looked at the mimosa tree. It was almost two-man heights and well-branched. It was in full blossom. This was a normal size for the tree, Latap thought. The tree Efum had chosen to hide Maru in must have been ancient, he thought, since she considered this one a baby tree. No wonder Efum told her "the spirit of the tree is protection." Even without the flowers, it would do a good job of hiding someone, especially if it were as well-spread as she described.

"No, Uncle. It makes me remember my father's words. My father wanted me and the people safe. He told me the spirit of that tree was protection. It protected me so I could return to warn you. We have come so very far. And here where we are to live is the tree, and the spirit of the tree is protection. It's as if my father knows we are safe here. It is a sign that says the protection we seek is here. Do you understand?"

Latap almost laughed aloud at her question, not one that children asked adults, but he did understand her asking. "Yes, Maru, I think I understand. You think this tree is a sign that this place is right. The people will have protection here. Are you suggesting that within this tree there is a spirit of protection for us?"

"I know of nothing else to think, Uncle. My father made such a point of it. It seems to have been the final point he made. We must be safe now. And this, our protection, stands proudly by Pedra Furada, in the spirit of this tree. As far as we traveled, there has not been another tree like this. But here, where we settle, the tree appears."

"I will think on this, Maru," Latap promised.

She nodded her head. Maru went to Pedra Furada and climbed to the hole. She wanted to walk about inside the hole. A cool breeze blew through her hair. Maru looked out over the land where rocks stood up, rocks such as the ones that made the caves her people would live in. She thought of her father. How she wished he could have seen this sight. Maybe he could see it from the place of the dead. She wondered. Maru was pleased. She looked down on the little protection tree. Her people needed it. It would be there forever, Maru hoped. She descended the rock wall to the ground. She had been inside Pedra Furada. The tree and the hole in the rock—both brought the day a wonderful experience for her. She returned home to see what she could do to help. Maru was healing, sporadically but definitely.

Gol called to Maru. She ran to him.

"Bring some small waterbags, he told her, and follow me. We have to walk a small distance to fill them," he told her.

Maru did as requested, but she thought it unusual for them to have moved to a place where water wasn't readily available on the site. Then, she remembered the tree, and her concern vanished.

The hunters returned in pairs over the afternoon. They had found two camels, a tapir, numbers of large lizards, and an anteater. By early evening the central outside cooking hearth was alive with the savor of meat cooking. A temporary place where the people would gather to eat and to assemble for council was established near the cave entrances.

Hunters had gone to the waterfall downhill to clean up after their butchering. All had returned. Chim was bandaging her son Moa's leg where he cut it on the hunt against a rock that he hadn't seen in his chase. It was a deep cut but appeared clean.

She put honey and herbs on the cut and wrapped it with leather. She warned him to have her clean it every day for the next five days.

Occasionally Bru would cough, and it was loud enough that all in the area could hear it. Each of the people saddened when they heard it. Bru had hung on so well through the long journey. They were hoping he'd improve now that the weather had warmed some, and they'd reached their destination. Magul had made a shelter for the old man at the back of the cave where they would live. Tamin helped her by laying the soft, furred skins on the vegetation they'd put down for softness. Then, Latap and Erru helped move Bru from the litter to his sleeping place. Bru objected but gave in when Latap and Erru promised to bring him to the eating and council place when the food was ready.

Maru told her brothers, Tau and Vale, about climbing to the hole. Both wanted to do the same thing. They had finished the work they had been told to do, so they headed for the opening in the rock. It took some time but all three arrived at the great hole. They were examining the place when Perru spotted them and ordered them down. Perru's legs were bothering him, but he watched until all three children were back on the ground. Then he told them they were not permitted to climb up there. At council, he would make that an order for children. Maru looked at Tau from the corner of her eye. They smiled slyly. They'd been there. They knew what it was like. Forbidden places always had a special attraction. Others might wonder; *they knew*.

As the sun set, the food was ready. After their travels, the meal was a feast. They ate more than their fill, and enjoyed every bite. Bru was elated to have survived to witness the event. The meat, especially the camel, was wonderful. After the meal was cleared away, council began.

Perru began as he usually did. "This is our first day and night in our new home. Before we discuss more serious matters, listen well children. Anyone less than fifteen years of age is not permitted to climb to the Pedra Furada. There are no exceptions. Anyone less than fifteen years of age caught at the hole up there will be punished severely. Are there any questions?"

No one made a sound. Only Maru and her brothers had yet thought to climb there. They would not go there again until they reached the age of fifteen. They could hardly wait to attain that age so they could go again. Those fifteen or over suddenly had an emerging interest to climb to the hole.

"For more serious matters," Perru continued. "Maru, listen well," he said.

Maru was startled. She hoped he wouldn't single her out for climbing Pedra Furada.

"You told of the tree where Efum hid you from the people at Molgray. You said he told you 'the spirit of the tree is protection.' Is that right?"

Maru nodded.

"Answer me, Girl," Perru said, short-tempered.

"Yes, Grandfather," she said loud enough that he could hear with ease.

"You showed Latap a tree like that one, only much smaller, that grows here. Is that right?"

"Yes, Grandfather," Maru replied.

"You see that as a sign that this place is our protection against harm. Is that right?"

"Yes, Grandfather."

"We men have discussed this. We agree. We consider the mimosa tree you found sacred."

Maru sat there with her mouth hanging open. She was amazed.

"We will care for the tree. We will provide it water in dry times. We will put forest floor vegetation around its base to feed it and to protect its roots. We will revere the tree. People, do not touch the tree. It is now sacred. When you look toward the tree, thank it for its spirit of protection. As long as the tree survives, we have protection. Is that understood?"

There was silence and nobody moved. The tree was declared sacred. That was a big thing for the people.

Perru continued, "There is one other thing that is sacred to us. It is the one thing that kept us alive on our long voyage. Who among you children knows what it is?"

Tab, Abut's eleven-year-old daughter, stood quickly. Perru said, "Tab?"

"I think it must be the crocodiles. Without them, we might have starved."

"Very good, Tab," Perru said.

Tab sat down.

"Now," Perru continued, "Mego."

Mego sat up straight. She had no idea what was coming.

"Mego, your painting has been sometimes trouble-some until now. You will paint a life-sized crocodile on the wall along our cave line. Be sure it is protected from rain. It must last a long time. Make sure it isn't like the things you used to paint that looked real. It's the spirit of the crocodile that is sacred to us, not the live ones. It is sacred as the tree is sacred, but the tree can live among us; crocodiles cannot. Because of the protection of the tree and the provision of the crocodiles, we will include them in our worship. As it is with the tree—nobody is permitted to touch it—so it is with the painting Mego will make. No one is to touch it. Are there any questions?

There were no questions.

"Latap?" Perru said, asking whether Latap had anything to say.

Latap rose. "I would ask the hunters to describe the conditions for hunts in the area."

Abut stood. "We saw a wide assortment of animals today within easy reach of our home. If things stay this way, we should have no problems with a supply of food. Mother has suggested we smoke jerky for times when there may be some difficulty finding food animals. My mother is a wise woman."

"I agree," Erru said, smiling at his wife. A few of the people laughed gently, aware that Erru probably meant that the smoked jerky was a good idea, and, that his wife was wise, were both true.

No one else had anything to ask or add, so the council broke up. People headed to their caves for the night. Moa and Lamut carried Bru to his bed. He asked Magul for the large gourd which he'd been using to relieve himself. She handed it to the old man. He used it and laid it beside him. Magul started to take it outside to empty it, but Fig stood quickly and took it from her. He carried it a good distance away and emptied it, brought it back, and placed it beside the old man.

Maru slipped into her sleeping place next to Tau. She was in wonder at the events of the evening. The special tree was pronounced sacred. The old ones understood what her father had told her. She would honor the tree for the rest of her days.

Just as all began to settle and sleep for the night, a moaned "No!" rent the night's silence.

Magul told those in her cave to remain still. She'd find out the reason for the sound.

Shortly she returned. Aps had lost the baby she carried. Magul had helped her with the delivery. The baby would have been a boy. Magul wrapped the baby in a soft leather, and put it beside the cave wall until daylight when Bid would bury it. Because of their prior losses of children, any loss of a child, whether born alive or dead, was considered a tragedy and there was a funeral. Tupal's funeral was just after his death. The dead baby would join Tupal in the ground the next day.

When Magul returned to her cave, most of her family slept. She whispered the dreadful news. Maru heard and tears leaked from her eyes. She was sad for Aps and for the people. It was different to her from the death of her father. He was someone she'd known all her life. The baby had never taken a breath. No one, unless it was Aps, knew him at all.

Still, he was one who would have been numbered among them but would not.

The people, with the exception of Bid and Aps, slept.

When the sun rose the people began to stir. Magul discovered that Bru no longer breathed. She couldn't bring herself to wail. The old man had told her his goal was to reach their new home so that he would sleep among his people. His cough and difficulty breathing were uncomfortable. She knew he died eager to see his wife again and happy to sleep among his people. She went to Perru and told him that Bru was gone.

The people ate and then Bid, Perru, Erru, Latap, Gol, and Abut all went to the burial area to dig graves for the oldest and the little one who did not live to breathe. It took a long time. Fig, Lamut, Moa, and Due gathered flat rocks and carried them to the graveside. They would lay rocks on all the graves to discourage animals at night from digging the bodies up.

While the men dug the graves, Femur and Tab climbed the hill to follow the bees they'd seen at the sacred tree. They wanted to locate the source of honey, so the hunters could supply the needs of the people. The women had indicated their honey supply was running low. It took a while, but finally they saw two bees heading from the tree in their direction. They followed them to a tree, and sure enough to the far side of a tree stump, they could hear the bees active inside. They marked the place so they could find it easily again.

Shortly after the girls returned home, each of the people walked around the grave in a complete revolution while taking their last look at the ones who died. Then, those who dug the graves filled them back with the dirt piles at the edge of the grave. People wept and moaned at the grave. Then, they left the area to resume the day. Women tried to comfort Aps. She was in more emotional than physical pain from her loss.

Mego asked her brother, Moa, to accompany her to the pool by the waterfall. She needed to gather some clay and heard there was some available downstream from the water source. Moa finished his part of stashing firewood in a rockshelter and joined her.

"I'm sorry I don't have the courage to go there myself. It's just too far for my voice to carry if there were trouble."

"It's my pleasure to go with you, Mego. I enjoy the walk there, and I am here to protect you whenever you feel a need. You said something about gray clay?"

"Yes. We don't have crocodiles here. The gray is for the spirit of the crocodile, not for real ones."

"Aren't crocodiles gray?"

"Yes. I'm hoping this one will be a paler gray. When people die their skin gets lighter. That's the effect I'm after."

"I understand. Won't the pale gray merge with the rock color?"

"It might, but I will use charcoal from the hearth fire to mark the edges of the crocodile. That way the colors won't merge."

"It seems you've thought of everything," Moa said smiling and thinking of how wonderful it was to have such an amazing sister.

Mego stopped walking. "Not really, Moa. There is a ledge available to stand on to paint, but it is very narrow. It will be dangerous."

"Do you have to paint there?"

"I've looked carefully at the available places. There is no better place to assure the painting remains long after we are dead."

Moa stood there looking at his sister. He hadn't grasped the full importance of the spirit crocodile. It was to protect the people and their children and their children's children and beyond for countless years after he breathed no longer. It was a tie for his people to protection by the crocodile spirit for as long as life was in that place. He thought that meant they'd never hunger. The crocodile spirit would protect them from hunger. He marveled that they could do something that would communicate over such a long time. He thought briefly and then said, "If you need a standing place, I can build you one. You tell me. Show me the place when we return."

"I will," she promised. Mego was delighted she'd shared with Moa. Her brother was a wonderful man, she thought. They continued on to the water source to gather gray clay.

"How will we show our respect for the tree?" Abut asked Latap and Gol.

"Well, we've already established that it cannot be touched because it's sacred," Gol replied.

"That doesn't seem enough to me," Latap said after some thought. "Remember how we worshipped the spirit of the great rock back home?"

"You mean the circling and singing of the song of praise or the washing of the rock?"

Latap said, "I was thinking of the circling of the rock and the song of praise to the spirit of the rock as we circled. That always meant so much to me. It was a ritual that I felt made me very close to the spirit of the rock."

"But only men participated in the spirit of the rock worship. That's because it looked like our manhood," Abut added.

"Well, the spirit of the tree is protection. That applies to all whether male or female, old or young or between," Gol said quietly.

"I can just imagine it," Abut said, "We circle singing, 'O, great spirit of protection, living in the mimosa tree ....' I am not a song maker."

Gol and Latap laughed over the addition to the song of "I am not a song maker."

"We can call on Mat for that," Gol said. "He makes songs."

"I think we should call on Erru also to guide the making of the circling," Latap said.

"Yes!" Gol replied with enthusiasm. "He would know just what to do."

"We have a plan?" Latap asked.

"Yes, we have a plan," the other two agreed.

"I'll talk to Erru," Gol said, since Erru was his father.

"I'll talk to Mat," Abut added, because Mat was his son.

The Boqueirão refuge was alive with activity. People had found a place to store jerky, and hunters were looking for likely jerky meat sources as well as food for the day. Those aged eleven to fourteen were scouring the area for fallen branches that would be good for hearth fires. They carried them to the rock-shelter to keep them from rain, to retard their rotting, and to make better fires. Girls were sent to find plants for their food at present and to dry for the winter. Tamin and Mu were busy mending and making new clothing. The voyage had been hard on the skins. Potu and Mu were making new sleeping skins as the hunters brought their kills. Older boys were butchering the meat and setting some up for jerky, while other meat was taken to Magul and Chim for the cooking hearth. Sue and Atella were assigned the task of keeping the children from two to five years old busy. Maru and Tero, both seven years old, had complained of being put with the little ones, and they were given permission to join with the older children to search for hearth firewood. Perru worked stone to create spear points, sitting to remove pressure from his knees.

Moa asked Due to join him at the wall where Mego wanted to paint the crocodile. Both were in agreement that the place was good, but it was well beyond her reach. The two men spent the afternoon in great thought. Finally they came up with the idea of building a long ladder. They'd need two strong tree trunks that would be made from tall trees, limbed, and set up with crosspieces to hold it firmly in shape. They'd have to cut down trees from the forest to build the ladder. They wanted to build a place near the top where Mego could stand and set gourds to hold the paint. After the painting was finished, they'd store the long logs for future use. They had plenty of cordage, but they asked Chim to make more, thicker cordage, because they'd never built a ladder, and they had no true idea how much cordage they'd need. The major concern was Mego's safety as she'd climb up and down and stand to paint. She was creative and understood things that were spiritual more acutely than any of the people. They had relied on Perru, but all knew she had a depth of spirit that Perru didn't have. Perru was the first to recognize and admit it. He would sometimes consult with her before council. She was at the edge of what the people considered sacred. It would not do at all for her to be injured, even for a painting that would outlive her.

Moa and Due carried their tools to a place beyond the water source. They could not remove trees near their home. Not only were the trees near their home too short, but also there was something built into their culture for longer than any of them were alive. There was something spiritual connected to trees. They did not want offended spirits of the trees near their living areas. They feared retribution.

They found trees that were roughly eight man-heights tall. They took their axes and slowly began to cut away at the trees. They knew how to cut the trees so they'd fall where they wanted. It took a good while for the first tree to fall. At the base it was three to four hand widths across, large trees. Moa did most of the cutting down of the first tree.

While Due began working on the other, Moa began to limb the tree that had already been dropped. He and Due limbed the second and then began to cut the trees so they would be as long as they desired, about four man heights. Moa measured, and Due was the standard of measure. They wanted the bases to be about the same size. One tree had to have more base removed and the other needed to be cut back at the top. Then began the work of hauling the tree home. They had to do it one tree at a time with help from others. It was strenuous.

It would take Moa and Due ten days to construct the ladder. They had to figure out how to create a device they could attach to the ladder, so that Mego had a place to stand and set the gourds for the gray and black paint.

While they built the ladder, Mego gathered animal fat from a daily kill and rendered it to make the additive to the charcoal for black and gray clay for the grayish-white mixture for the spiritual nature of the crocodile. She also found a large shoulder bone from the bone storage for a surface to grind the charcoal to powder. She had two gourds she had from their former home to hold the clay and powder until she was ready to mix them with the rendered fat. She ground the charcoal finely and placed it in the gourd.

"That stinks!" Maru teased Mego. "Can't you do that somewhere else?"

Mego smiled at Maru, "Well, I thought of moving it to the place just in front of your cave, where the ground is amazingly flat, but I decided rendering the fat here would keep the odor down."

The two girls laughed. Odors weren't something that the people were much concerned about. They were aware that some things required odor—just part of life. Rendering fat wasn't, however, very appealing.

The people were becoming fascinated with the construction of the ladder, examining it daily. Because of the weight of the ladder, Moa and Due placed each tree against the wall where the ladder would be set. They dug spots on the ground into which they inserted the tree base so that it wouldn't slide. As they worked, they checked with Mego to assure their placement was good for her plans.

Moa and Due spent the day after they brought the two tree trunks home gathering crosspieces. They found small trees they could cut down near the big ones they'd already taken. Fig, Mat, and Tab joined them and carried back crosspieces as they cut them. It took a full day to gather as many of them as planned. If Moa and Due had any left over, they would put them with the hearthfire wood the people had collected. Chim gave Moa a large amount of heavy duty cordage to attach the crosspieces.

After the morning meal, Due and Moa began to place the crosspieces on the tree trunks starting at the bottom. They tried, whenever possible, to rest the crosspiece on a cut off limb for additional sturdiness. Their goal was to make equal distances between the crosspieces. Sometimes in the absence of an appropriately level branch extension, they'd loop cordage over a cut off tree limb extension higher up and wrap cordage around it and the tree trunk until it met the crosspiece at the lower level. Again, this was their way to assure additional sturdiness of the crosspiece. Under no circumstances did they want the crosspiece to slip. They chuckled to themselves that they'd not have even considered taking these precautions, if they were the ones to use the ladder. For Mego, on the other hand, it had to be perfect.

When they reached what they thought half the required crosspieces, they called Mego.

When she arrived, Due asked her, "Will you climb as high as you can go to let us know whether the ladder seems comfortable to you?"

Mego climbed up the ladder until her hands reached the top crosspiece. She had no problem with the ladder.

Due and Moa continued adding crosspieces. Finally, they reached the top. Due called Mego who came promptly to see what they wanted of her.

"Will you climb again to the top this time?" Moa asked. "The piece we'll add for you to stand on isn't made yet, but we want to know how well you do on the ladder."

Mego climbed the ladder and a little over halfway up her knees began to shake, for the ladder had a little bounce to it. She called down, "Is this ladder going to break?"

Moa replied, "No, at that distance up, there is a little flexibility in the wood. Don't look down; just go on up."

Mego had lost her nerve. The ladder was positioned in exactly the right place for the best location to paint the crocodile. She tried to focus on the task, but the flexing of the ladder frightened her terribly. Slowly, Mego descended.

"I have to cure my fright," she explained.

"Mego, what causes your fright?" Due asked with concern.

"I don't know," she replied vaguely.

Due looked at her long enough for her to look directly into his eyes. "If you don't know what's causing the fright, Mego, how do you plan to solve the problem? You cannot wait for a long time while the ladder remains raised, causing a hazard." His voice had a slight edge.

"I don't know," she said, tears leaking from her eyes and rivering through the dust on her face.

"Do you think the ladder will fall?" Moa asked with consideration.

"I don't know," she said, her hands moving against each other.

"Pay attention, Mego," Moa demanded, frustrated with her vagueness.

Frightened of becoming a little unnerved by Moa, Mego paid attention. Moa walked deliberately over to the ladder. He climbed up the ladder, which bounced a little when he reached the place where she had found her knees shaking. He continued up all the way to the top. He came down to the ground.

"Watch again, Mego," Moa demanded sternly, and he repeated his climb.

Moa walked over to Mego and grabbed her by the arm, jerking her up. "Now, climb up the ladder all the way to the top. Do it now. Don't look down. Don't stop until you reach the top." His words were demanding, harsh, giving no room for argument.

Mego felt him release her arm. His finger shapes remained on her arm. She had never seen her brother so angry. She went to the ladder and climbed all the way to the top.

While she went to the ladder, Due whispered, "What's wrong with you?" He betrayed his astonishment in his voice.

"I'm just trying to cause her to be more afraid of me than of the ladder. She has to climb it. She must find courage."

Then she came down. On the ground, she breathed a sigh of relief. She could do it. She walked over to Moa and said, "Why do you hate me?"

"I don't hate you, Mego. I wanted you to see that your fear took away your courage. Life requires courage. You feared me more than you feared the ladder. You should have learned something. What did you learn?"

"I learned that the ladder isn't going to break."

"Long before you finish painting the crocodile, my sister, you'll have no fear whatsoever of the ladder."

"You promise?" she asked, still a little shaky.

"Yes, I promise."

"Moa and Due," she said quietly, "near the place where my legs shake, the ladder is too far from the wall for me to paint. Can you push the ladder closer when I reach that need?"

"We will find a way, when that time comes," he assured her. "Mego, stay off the ladder unless you have men around for safety." He turned from her to gather more of the crosspieces to take to the covered area where they were keeping wood for the hearth.

Fig found Moa and Due after the evening meal. "Have you figured out how to make a platform for the ladder?" he asked.

"We plan to discuss it tomorrow," Due told him. "Do you have information that can help us?" Due asked.

"I have some thoughts. I don't know how helpful it will be, but I'd like to share." Fig was a little intimidated by Moa and Due. They weren't significantly different in age, but Fig felt the difference.

"Please share with us," Moa asked. "We have put off planning this part because it's difficult."

"I uh, well, I think that triangles are strong," Fig began. "If you can find a tree limb that bends like this (Fig formed his arm in a right angle) and at the other end it branches again. Think of it as a spear haft. You can cut the bottom as you would cut a spear haft and bind it so it won't split further. You attach each end to a crosspiece that is separate from the ladder. The crosspieces should fit inside the tree trunks to prevent slipping. You'd want the leather strips damp so they dry tight. Let me draw this." He drew this in the sand:

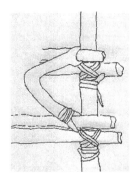

"Then, you have to bind the triangle to the two separate crosspieces. It would be good to use glue and leather as we do when hafting. Once you've done that to one side of the ladder, you do the exact same thing on the other side of the ladder. Then you attach another crosspiece above the bend. Like this:"

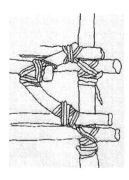

"At this point you add the platform for Mego to stand on and to hold the paint. Add crosspieces that are smaller than the one at the elbow. Put them close together so Mego's feet don't slide between them. Then, when you've finished both sides, you have a platform you can move up or down the ladder. You tie it to the ladder above the crosspieces at the top and the bottom. There are four attachments, two on each end. Attach the platform to the crosspiece and to the trunk of the tree. It should be strong enough and hold the gourds of paint."

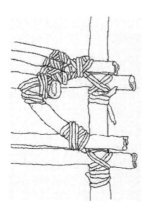

Moa and Due had watched the progression of the drawing carefully. Both were not only impressed with Fig's solution to the problem that had plagued them, but also they were amazed at his ability to illustrate something that complex, so they could understand.

"Fig, you solved our problem. This is wonderful! You did well. Please leave your drawing so we can use it, if we need to. I'll warn people at council to avoid disturbing the drawing."

Fig was turning red from the praise. He was not accustomed to anyone's praising him or blushing. It pleased him and made him feel most peculiar all at the same time. He looked up and said, "When

Mego prepares to paint, she should tie herself to the ladder, one tie to each side, I think."

"Thank you, Fig. You have solved another problem we hadn't even considered," Due said, clearly impressed. "What will be a challenge is finding those two elbows so they match. Want to go with us to help?" Moa asked.

To be asked to join with people of Moa and Due's stature was an enormous honor to Fig. Moa and Due were only three years older than Fig, but the two of them were seasoned hunters, esteemed by all. "I would be honored," Fig replied.

"We'll leave after the morning meal," Due told him.

Gol had talked to Erru, his father, about the ritual for worship of the mimosa tree. Abut had asked his son Mat to make a song for the worship. Both Mat and Erru had been thinking about the requests. Mat had made some progress. Erru had asked Mat to let him know when he had the song. He felt he could develop a proper tradition better, if he knew the song they'd sing.

Later Mat saw Gol at the wall where Mego would paint the crocodile spirit image. He went over to let him know he'd completed the song.

Gol looked at the wall and the ladder Due and Moa had built. It was well done. He knew they were working to build a standing place for Mego. He found it all very interesting.

"Gol, may I speak with you?" Mat asked the older man.

"Of course, Mat. Have you finished the song?"

"That's what I wanted to discuss with you. I have made a song, but I want you to tell me what you think. Do you have time now?"

"Of course," the older man said, crossing his feet and sitting on the ground. Mat sat down facing him and began to sing:

Efum was our great protector.

He knew the mimosa tree spirit, protection.

Efum was our great protector.

We fled our old home for this place.

The spirit of protection awaited us.

Efum knew you would be here waiting.

O, spirit of protection, we praise you.

Keep us safe in this new land.

Guard us from the evil of the sky.

Guard us from the evil of the land.

Guard us from the evil of the beast.

Guard us from the evil of the human.

Protect us from your wrath.

We praise you, O spirit of the mimosa tree, our protection.

When Mat finished, he was edgy. He wondered how Gol would respond. Gol asked him to sing it again, so Mat did.

Gol took his time thinking on the song. Then he said. "I think you made a perfect song. Now I can work on the tradition circle to accompany the tradition song."

Mat was relieved and delighted. He'd never been told a song was perfect. He rubbed his arms with the palms of his hands. Perfect! Hearing "perfect" was a feeling like being close to an explosive lightning strike that rushed over him when he heard the words, and made some of his hairs stand on end. Making the song right, especially this song, was very important to him. It was the most important song he'd ever make.

Gol worked on the tradition circle. What he devised was similar to the tradition circle the men had around the rock back at home. In this case, he understood, all the people would participate, not just the men. Gol worked out the tradition circle in this manner:

Gol said, "Men perform this ritual. We will have Erru keep the count with the drum. He will stand on the high ground. He will beat three beats, and then the ritual begins. Outside the circle of men is a circle of women and children and anyone else who cannot move with ease, like Perru. They circle to the left slowly during the whole song. They move the right foot over the left, move left foot from behind, and step left, then repeat."

Here's what the men do:

(Kneel, lift arms skyward.) Efum was our great protector. (Circle right to the count of four.)

(Prostrate self with head toward tree.) He knew the spirit of the mimosa tree, protection. (Circle to right, count of four.)

(Kneel, lift arms.) Efum was our great protector. (Circle right, count of four.)

(Kneel, lift arms.) We fled our old home for this place. (Circle right, count of four.)

(Prostrate self with head toward tree.) The spirit of protection awaited us. (Circle right, count of four.)

(Kneel, lift arms.) Efum knew you would be here waiting. (Circle right, count of four.)

(Prostrate self with head toward tree.) O, spirit of protection, we praise you. (Circle right, count of four.)

(Kneel, lift arms.) Keep us safe in this new land. (Circle right, count of four.)

(Kneel, lift arms.) Guard us from the evil of the sky. (Circle right, count of four.)

(Kneel, lift arms.) Guard us from the evil of the land. (Circle right, count of four.)

(Kneel, lift arms.) Guard us from the evil of the beast. (Circle right, count of four.)

(Kneel, lift arms.) Guard us from the evil of the human. (Circle right, count of four.)

(Kneel, lift arms.) Protect us from your wrath. (Circle right, count of four.)

(Prostrate self with head toward tree.) We praise you, O spirit of the mimosa tree, our protection. (Remain prostrate, count of thirteen.)

Gol asked Mat to practice the tradition with him. Mat would sing and Gol would show him the tradition circle. They went to the tree careful not to approach too closely. Gol knelt and Mat knelt and Mat began the song. They went through the entire song three times.

"I like it," Mat said with enthusiasm.

"The full moon is three days away," Gol said. "We can try to have our first worship then. After that we can repeat the tradition every thirteen days."

"That sounds wonderful," Mat replied.

"I'll ask at council whether that meets approval," Gol said sounding hopeful.

"I cannot think there would be any problem."

"Nor I, Mat, but it's always important to ask." Mat's reply bordered on vague as he gazed at the mimosa tree, caught up in the concept of protection.

There was a lot of practice in the next three days to prepare the worship tradition so all could remember what to do. Gol knew there would be a few people who had to watch others, but eventually all would learn it, so it would be routine.

By the evening of the third day, Moa and Due along with Fig had built the platform from which Mego could paint the crocodile. It was an exciting time. They were delighted to see new traditions forming to bring a cohesiveness to their group. This place, they were convinced, was a great blessing to the people. In this place, the people of Molgray would never find them. For that they had a deep sense of gratitude.

Their food stores were building up for the winter or times when animals were scarce. The supply of skins was growing and those who desperately needed clothing replacement had been accommodated. Women were also providing for those who needed clothing, but were not in critical need. Sleeping skins were replaced. Mego had her pigments ready for mixing with fat. The ladder and standing place were ready. The day after the ritual, she would begin to paint.

The evening of the new circle-song tradition arrived. Women prepared a feast for the occasion. The worship would follow the feast. Every delightful food filled the log where the food for the evening meal awaited the hungry people. Finally,

Perru called and all lined up to eat. Each person had a wooden wooden bowl. Each one picked up his or her bowl at the beginning of the line. Women served the food they requested in their bowls. Children were expected to choose a balance of foods. If they did not, the women would add whatever the children chose to ignore, usually vegetable in quantity. Children learned fast to choose well, for they had to eat what was in their bowl.

The people had practiced the worship song and movement for days. They were ready for the first expression of their worship of the tree of protection. There was a seriousness during the evening meal and a sense of urgency finally to perform the new ritual. Men envisioned themselves singing and making the movements, assuring that all would go well. Directly after eating, some of the women took the youngest children aside to assure that they understood the stepping to the left for their circle. They watched as the little ones put their right foot over their left foot and then brought the left foot from behind to step to the left. Then the right foot would cross over again and the left foot would follow. This was the first time all the people would participate in a ritual and the women definitely wanted to be sure all went well.

Finally, just before the sunset, it was time for the initial ritual. Everyone gathered around the tree with men forming the inner circle and women, children, and Perru forming the outer circle. The women, children, and Perru all joined hands. Erru beat the drum three times. At the fourth beat, the outer circle began to turn to the left while the men in the inner circle knelt and lifted their arms skyward, singing, "Efum was our great protector." While the outer circle continued stepping to the left at the drumbeats, the men circled to the right to the count of four. The men prostrated themselves with their heads toward the tree. They sang, "He knew the spirit of the mimosa tree, protection." They began the circle to the right to the count of four. This tradition was similar to their circle around the stone in their old homeland. That tradition was a male fertility ritual. Some of the men were becoming erect. A few noticed, but it did not bother anyone that this occurred. It was a normal thing for men, but it did come as a surprise that it occurred at this time. The people ignored it. The men in the inner circle knelt and lifted their arms skyward. They sang, "Efum was our great protector." While the outer circle continued its constant movement to the left, the men circled to the right to the count of four. They sang, "We fled our old home for this place." The men circled right to the count of four. They sang and performed the ritual carefully to its end. Then while the outer circle continued its leftward revolution, the men remained prostrate to the count of thirteen. The outer circle stopped with the last drum beat. The men slowly stood. They were very quiet, reflecting.

Erru had been the only one to see the ritual, since he was beating the drum while standing on higher land and could look down on the performance. He was so touched that tears leaked from his eyes and curved through the dust on his face. He was certain the spirit of the tree accepted the ritual. He was also certain that the Creator approved. They moved to the evening council and Erru told the people what he thought. The council ended and people dispersed to their homes, pleased with themselves.

As the sun rose and people began to prepare to eat the morning meal, Mego was as excited as she had ever been. It was the day she'd begin painting the sign of the crocodile protection that saved the people from starvation as they traveled the long river to their new home. She no longer feared the ladder greatly, having climbed it several times. She did, however, have a respect for what could happen, if she were careless while using the ladder.

After eating, Mego went to her ground charcoal and the clay she'd carefully kept wet. She had placed both pigments in the gourds she painstakingly guarded for her painting. She'd had the gourds as a youngster, seven years before the move, when she began to paint at the age of five years old. Mego carefully put some clay and some of the rendered fat into the gourd and gently stirred the mixture with a smooth stick. The gourd was large, so she had plenty of charcoal paint, enough to finish the whole task. She took the wet clay and put a large piece into the second gourd. She stirred fat into the clay. It was not as easily stirred as the charcoal powder and fat mixture. The stick she used to stir broke, so she used her hands to mix the two substances. She had to add additional fat. Finally, the mixture suited her. Mego wiped her hands on one of the extra pieces of leather she'd taken from the supply pile the women placed in baskets for undesignated future uses. She carried the gourds toward the ladder. She'd have to go near the top of the ladder to reach the place where she planned to start—the crocodile's head. Moa had already secured the platform exactly where she wanted it.

Before she did anything else, Mego walked to the left of the ladder. She found a place on the wall like the one where she'd paint. She put her fingers into the gourd with the black paint. She pressed her fingers against the wall. Mego smiled looking at the effect. She tried the gray paint. It was also effective. Mego watched to be sure the paint remained on the wall. She returned to the ladder with a hint of a smile.

Moa and Due saw her heading to the ladder. "Wait, Mego!" Due shouted.

She stopped and turned to look at them.

"We will stay by the ladder while you paint. You go on up and tie yourself to the ladder like we showed you," Moa told her.

"And I'll carry the gourds up to you once you're there," Due added, holding out his hands for the gourds.

Mego nodded and put the gourds on the ground. She climbed the ladder and tied herself to each side of the tree trunks. Due was coming up with the first gourd. He placed it to the side of the standing place and went to pick up the second gourd. He came up with it and set it on the same side of the standing place. Then he joined Moa at the bottom of the ladder where they would watch over Mego as she painted.

Mego studied the wall carefully. She decided she would start the crocodile snout between the two tree trunks as high up as she could reach. The trunks would provide a good guide for her work. She would paint the crocodile from snout at the top to tail at the bottom as if she were perched in a tree looking down on the animal, and she considered, if she were near a live crocodile, she'd be very happy to be perched in a tree. The crocodile would seem to hang from the wall. Certainly the crocodiles gave their lives so her people didn't starve, but they were very dangerous animals. She didn't want her image to appear dangerous. Erru still had a big scar on his leg where one of the largest crocodiles hit him with a back foot. Erru said it was the animal's toenail that did it. Mego remembered it took a long time to heal. The infection was bad. Lamut had puncture marks on his arm. He'd been bitten. Erru and Gol had poked at the crocodile's eyes to make it let go of Lamut's arm. They killed that crocodile after they blinded it, because it would be cruel to let it starve and suffer.

Mego took a handful of the gray clay mixture and placed it on the wall just about as high as she could reach between the tree trunk sides of the ladder and between the crosspieces of the ladder. She smeared the color into the wall with her fingers. She smiled when she discovered that the paint didn't run down the wall but rather stuck as she hoped it would. Encouraged, she took more paint and applied it, patiently pressing it deeply into the surface of the wall. When she finished the snout, she had to climb down to make more paint. She began to untie herself.

"What are you doing, Mego?" Due asked.

"I have to make more paint," she replied.

"Is it something we can do?" Moa asked, eager to do anything rather than stand around.

"No," she replied, continuing to untie herself.

Due had started up the ladder. He reached out for the gourd, and Mego handed it to him with a twisted smile. She was comfortable with the thought of ascending and descending the ladder while holding the gourd. *Did they think I can't go up and down the ladder carrying something? Why?* She wondered, almost but not quite irritated. According to Due and Moa, she was to use two hands going up and coming down. She accepted their rules, though she felt the rules were unnecessary.

She went quickly to the place where she took more clay and added the fat. She didn't even try mixing it with a stick but rather used her hands to combine the clay and fat. Then she wiped her hands on the piece of leather she'd used earlier. She hurried back to the ladder and her task. She climbed up and Moa brought the gourd to her as she tied herself to the ladder. Mego continued to apply the gray mixture to the snout and down onto the space where she planned to paint the head. She went from reaching high to kneeling on the platform. She had covered the area of the snout to the slight indentation for the crocodile's neck.

Mego untied herself from the ladder and began to descend.

"Are you finished for today?" Due asked.

"No. I need to come down to see from a distance."

"Well, that makes sense," Moa said, considering what she'd said.

Mego laughed out loud. "Of course, it makes sense!" she muttered to herself.

She walked a good distance from the base of the ladder. She studied the image carefully and found that she was pleased with what she'd done. She climbed back up and took the other gourd.

"You've forgotten to tie yourself to the ladder," Moa reminded her. He thought that there was good reason he and Due were standing at the base of the ladder, watching.

Mego put the gourd down and tied herself to the ladder. She picked up the gourd with her black paint, and, taking less of it on her fingers than she took when painting the gray, she began to outline the gray head and snout. She made the outline touch the gray paint that seemed almost dry. She wanted the crocodile to stand out visually. She quietly hummed to herself the tune of the last night's tradition song for the spirit of protection of the mimosa tree. She went again from a position of stretching to paint the snout to bending down to reach the edge of the neck. When she finished the outline, Mego put the paints down, untied herself from the ladder, and came down.

"I need to move further down," she told Moa and Due.

Due went up and took both gourds and returned to the ground. While he put them aside, Moa climbed up to untie the standing place to move it down the ladder. He was unsure whether to move it down two or three crosspieces. He tied it two crosspieces down. Once it was secured, Mego tried the new level. It was satisfactory, she decided. She retied herself and went back to the painting.

Mego knew the crocodile narrowed where the legs attached. Its belly bulged out to the side somewhere between two and three times the size of its head in width. She took the gray clay paint and extended it from the neck past the arms to the sides of the belly and carried it as far down as she could. The standing place would have to move, she realized, before she could paint the whole body.

She stood on the platform for a while. Gray clay dropped slowly from her hand to accumulate on the platform. She decided she could paint the outline of the crocodile with gray. She could paint some vertical lines on the crocodile's mid-section to represent the lines formed on the crocodile's back from the scaly plates. Then between the gray vertical lines and the animal's sides, she'd add some dots to show the rounded protrusions on the crocodile that formed between the scales of the top of its back down the sides toward the underbelly. She felt very satisfied. She remembered a lot about the crocodile but not how many lines ran vertically. Rather than strive for perfection, she could use the lines to represent imperfectly remembered details with as much fact as she remembered perfectly. The people would understand. She knew they'd have no failure understanding her painting.

Mego took some more gray paint and reached out to paint the front legs. She couldn't reach the wall.

She called to Moa and Due and told them the problem. Moa climbed up the ladder and it began to bend closer to the place she needed to reach. It was just a bit short.

"I'm heavier than you are," Due said. "Come down and I'll climb up there."

Moa descended and Due climbed up. It worked. Mego hurried to paint the sides, the vertical lines along the back and the dots with gray. Then, she took the black and made the outline. She painted the front legs of the crocodile, as if they reached high forward up the wall. She couldn't reach as far as necessary to paint the whole leg on either side. The ladder would need to move or a different platform would be necessary. She wiped the gray on the leather and took the charcoal paint. Carefully she outlined what she could reach on either side of the legs. When she had done all she could, she went back down the ladder.

"I have to look at it from a distance," she explained before they asked.

She walked away from the ladder and looked up.

"Looks good to me," Gol said as he passed by.

"Thank you," Mego replied with a grin for Gol. She liked it also, but she would never have said that.

When she returned to the ladder she told Moa that the platform needed to move down three crosspieces. She'd painted as far down as she could possibly reach by bending down, sometimes lying down flat on the platform and reaching far below.

Moa climbed up to retrieve the gourds, and Due climbed up to move the standing place as soon as Moa was back on the ground.

Mego continued working until she had finished painting and adding more dots with gray. Then, she outlined the gray of the animal with black. All that remained were the legs. She added the gray of the rear legs painting them as if they reached up from the crocodile body toward the front of the beast. She outlined the gray with black paint. Then she climbed back down.

The three of them went to the cooking hearth. They were hungry and thirsty.

Moa and Due had been solving the problem of extending the ladder so she could reach the ends of the crocodile legs. They'd tie two extra-long logs to the standing place where Mego could exceed the width of the ladder to reach to paint the animal's legs. They'd also tie an extra-long crosspiece to the trunks so she had something to hold onto while she painted. She'd definitely have to remember to tie herself to the ladder. They knew this would be the most dangerous part of her painting from the ladder.

After they ate, Moa and Due moved the standing place lower so that Mego could finish the crocodile to the end of its tail. It took a few more moves down the ladder. She worked diligently to do the best possible work she could. She took the time required for the wall to absorb the paint fully before pushing on.

She felt a bond with the wall and paint that would last longer than she would, as if it captured part of her seventh soul to share with the images she would paint. This was a sacred task and she never forgot that. When she'd painted all she could paint within the confines of the two trunks of the ladder, Moa took the extra-long crosspieces up and tied them to the platform which had been moved to enable her to finish the front legs. Mego painted three toes on each foreleg, but only outlined the outside edges of the first and third toes. She would do the same with the front and back toes.

Due moved the standing place with the extra-long crosspieces down two crosspieces on the ladder and Mego painted the remaining legs, still aiming forward, as if the crocodile hung from the rock wall. Mego added only three toes to each foot, not recalling that they had five. She did not remember the webbing was greater on the back rather than front feet. Using charcoal paint, Mego outlined the exterior edges of the first and third toes only. Then she descended the ladder. She walked away from the ladder and turned back to look.

Mego was pleased with the painting. Painting it in the light gray instead of the darker gray had been a good idea. It was recognizable to her people clearly as spirit and not physical substance. It seemed about the right size for a large crocodile, but not the largest. The work had been a challenge, but she'd met the challenge. A small smile played at the edges of her lips. She liked what she saw.

Perru came over to her and put his hand on her shoulder. "You've done a very good painting, Mego. I'm proud of you. Between the tree and this painting we are establishing ourselves here. It is very good to have these things."

Mego smiled at him. He had made happiness sing within her.

Moa and Due gathered the parts of the ladder as they began to disassemble it. While Moa untied the crosspieces, Due took them to a space in a rock-shelter where they planned to keep the ladder.

Mego went to the quick wash container to clean her hands. She took some of the rendered fat and rubbed it on her hands. Her work had dried them. By the time the evening meal was ready, the crocodile had been painted and the ladder was placed at the rockshelter along with the standing place which they did not disassemble.

At council that night, Perru said, "Every time you look at the crocodile that Mego painted today, take a moment to thank the crocodile for giving itself to us so that we didn't starve on our way here. Pray to the spirit of the crocodile to keep our bellies filled while we live in this wonderful new land.

All of the people said, "I will!"

Part 3

Two years passed since the people moved to the Boqueirão refuge. The people had settled down to a routine. Babies were born; there were no other deaths than Tupal, the oldest elder, Bru, and Aps and Bid's baby, who never breathed. Hunters hunted; women made clothing and food; children learned the ways of the people. Outside of the routine were the activities of Mego and Fig. Mego had made the first painting in gratitude and remembrance of the spirit of the crocodile who gave itself in numbers, so the people didn't starve as they traveled to the new land. The people still invoked protection from hunger, when viewing the image of the crocodile on the wall. When others learned of Fig's ability to make images in the dirt, they encouraged him also to paint. The two painters spent some of their time painting. If a hunt was significantly successful, either Mego or Fig might paint a hunter and the animal killed on the wall. They might also paint an image of one of the local animals that was their primary food source for multiple reasons. When other spirits were helpful to the people, one of the painters would paint a representation of the spirit on the wall.

The wall was becoming an important part of their culture. At council they spoke of the wall as a way to communicate praise of the spirits and significance of events relating to their lives for the present and for future people long after those of the current generation left for the spirit world. Others said that during their own lifetimes the wall would hold memory that otherwise the people would forget. The entire wall was given sacred status. The people were not allowed to touch the paintings once they were completed.

There was a certain pride of community and to a far lesser degree of pride of the person. When Gop or Potu made an especially serviceable garment, or Due speared a saber tooth cat alone, they triumphed for the moment, but it was fleeting. They gained no status. Their status was not individual focused but rather group oriented, a very effective and happy community of people who worked to keep it that way. They decorated the wall to glorify their community not set one person above another. That's why Erru, the oldest of the elders, was shocked at Perru's question.

"My Brother," Erru replied slowly, clearly surprised. "That is not our way. Why would you want to change it?"

"What do you mean, it's not our way? We glorified the spirit of the crocodile, and there's a deer painted over there."

"We have no images of any specific person on the wall."

"Of course we do. When Due speared the saber tooth cat, Fig painted him on the wall."

"He painted a hunter, not Due. Show me anything that makes that Due. The hunter could be anyone. Fig knows better than to glorify a man."

"Well, I think Gol deserves to be on the wall after the way he brought us safely here. This is a great place to live. I much prefer it to the jungle."

"I'm completely against it, but I'll bring it up at council." Erru shook his head slightly and walked away.

It was time to eat the evening meal, so the people rapidly went to their gathering place for eating. After the meal, before they cleared away the food, Erru said that there had been only one issue for council, and he'd like to discuss it. The people quickly reconfigured their seating for council and looked at Erru.

"I have been asked to have an image of a specific person painted on the wall. I want to know how you feel about that. If a hunter makes an extremely good kill, should the hunter be identified on the wall? Bid, for example, wears that leather bracelet. Moa has a necklace. Sometimes Gol braids a feather into his hair. Should we give prominence to these things or treat all the people the same?"

Gol stood up. "I think we should all be treated the same. We don't put people above others as the

Molgray did. No one here is any better than another. Paintings are powerful. We've already learned that. I would not want to be painted up there to be identified personally. I think it would be wrong and cause division among us." He went back to his seat. Gol had no idea that Perru wanted to have an image of him on the wall. He'd have been horrified.

"It's an interesting idea," Lamut added, not rising but rather remaining seated, "but I agree with Gol. It could create divisions among us. That would not be good."

There was silence.

"Well, I think it's a good idea," Perru said, standing and walking closer to the older people. "It could become like a reward for exceeding expectations."

Mu, Abut's wife stood. She wasn't free to speak out but rather waited to be acknowledged.

"Mu." Erru gave her the authorization to speak.

"I have much time spent with all of the people from the tiny ones to the middle ages to those who are adults to the elders. There is not a single group where it is a good idea to raise one above others. It brings out an attack response in those who develop jealousy, and for those who are finding their places, it can be dispiriting. For those who seem elevated, it brings out a sense of thinking more of themselves than they should. For humans it is not a good thing suggested here. Not at any age." Mu returned to her seat.

The absolute silence was unexpected. Mu knew the ways of the people. She taught everyone. People confided their thoughts to her, for she was trusted not to divulge any disclosure. Her advice was frequently sought. Way off in the distance there was trumpeting from either a mammoth or gomphothere.

Now was the time to call for the people to let their choice be known, Erru thought. All people age fifteen and above participated. He hoped the people would remember the words just spoken by Mu.

"If you think painters should personalize people, please stand," Erru said and sat down. Perru with his bad knees was already standing. Erru waited. No one else at council stood. The place was deadly quiet, utterly unmoving.

"The people have made it clear. We continue as we have been. People will not be personalized in paintings. That is all."

As the people filed out to finish cleaning up from the evening meal, Fig and Bid headed to the highest hill. They were the night watch. There had been some migrations since the people arrived. During some of the migrations, animals came through their community in the outside living place and caused occasional destruction. Since then, a night watch had been set up. For migrations it was possible to turn a herd by holding up branches of trees to head them in different directions. This was helpful, they learned, in the hunt as well as the protection of the community. The men also watched for anything that might be out of the ordinary. Watchers stood on the highest ground.

"This won't be much fun tonight," Fig said. "You see that lightning?"

"It was such a little one I wasn't sure that's what I saw."

"We should have quite a storm later, if I'm interpreting the clouds right," Fig added.

"We'll see," Bid replied. Bid had been arguing with Aps over whose fault it was that they only had one child, while others had several. Aps felt it was her fault somehow, but she couldn't reason why. Bid wasn't interested in fault, and assured her that things were what they were. He wanted her to return to her happy self. Something happened to her at the death of their first baby, he thought. She'd never been the same after that. Aps and Bid's smaller number of children did not reflect positively or negatively on either one of them, he knew, but she doubted. They tried to be the best parents they could be. To Bid that was all that was important. He felt he'd never understand Aps. He loved her. That was clear, but, he thought, life with a woman was tough. He was convinced she thought less of herself than she should. There seemed nothing he could do to change that.

Fig sat cross-legged on the skin he brought. He hadn't carried with him a large skin to protect him from the weather, because the day had been so warm. He stared off into the distance where the lightning continued to show forth gaining greater strength. Fig was a contented man. He listened for the thunder and thought he could hear an occasional rumble, though it was far away.

Bid paced back and forth slowly, somewhat distracted. He didn't discuss his problems with others, and Fig didn't pry. Each left the other to their own little worlds. As time passed, Fig stretched out on his back to watch the stars move through the sky. It was a pattern repeated nightly. He never tired of the sight.

Finally Fig sat up. Bid had settled down and was kneeling, while sitting on his heels. His head was down as if he napped. Fig squinted into the distance. The storm was moving closer, but under the storm there was a horizon of red. The sun didn't set over there, so Fig continued to watch to see what caused the red. It entered his thoughts that the red might be fire set off by lightning, but he wasn't ready to come to that conclusion. Fig had never seen a fire set by lightning. If it were fire, he was certain there would be plenty of time to warn the people.

He watched, and Bid continued to doze. Occasionally, Bid would topple to one side or the other, but he'd catch himself just as he was about to reach the point where he could no longer right himself. Fig was fascinated. At last, Fig poked Bid's arm.

"I think the storm has started a fire beyond the forest," Fig said.

Bid woke up quickly. He looked out and saw the fire approaching. The storm was throwing great bolts of lightning and making resonant thunderous noise they could feel in their bodies. Rain was beginning to fall sporadically.

"I will warn the people," Bid said and began to leave.

Bid ran quickly to the little community to find Erru. Erru waked up and immediately grabbed his spear and followed Bid. At the top of the hill where Fig had been watching, Erru looked out.

"Look at that!" Fig shouted pointing off to the side. A whirl of wind swooped down and gathered up fire, twisting it into a fire tornado. The fire went all the way from the burning red of the visible horizon to the cloud bottom. The sight was exquisitely beautiful and terrifying all at the same time. In a fascinating way it made Fig think of an evil spirit rising. Arriving at the overlook Erru noticed that horizontally there was a band of fire and vertically a great vortex of the red-orange-yellow flames with a pale rufous tinge on the bottoms of the clouds. Erru was startled by the sight. In his thoughts, he compared the fire tornado to a whirlpool of water running down a hole.

Erru took over. "Fig, go home and send the people to climb the hill above our homes. There is little vegetation there. Tell them to carry skins for protection with them. Bid, have a few of the men to gather skins, soak them, and cover the sacred tree top as well as possible. Yes, they'll have to touch the tree. Wrap the trunk and cover the roots with soaking wet skins."

Fig had already left at a fast run. "I will," Bid acknowledged the order, running right behind Fig who had neglected to acknowledge Erru's order.

Erru stood, watching the fire tornado. He'd never seen such a thing and though it was utterly fascinating, he hoped never to see one again. Erru stood on the top of the hill with his arms raised high. "Creator, protect us from this fire. What you made, you can protect. Hold your hand up so the flames stop before they reach the waterfall, pond, and our river. Hear me, Creator. Hear my cry for help. We are but few in this great land. Protect us!" Though the cool rain was falling, sweat poured from Erru. He hoped with a desperation he'd never known that the Creator would hear him and protect them.

Not knowing what else to do, Erru went back to the Boqueirão refuge and began to search each cave area carefully. He found Hun in his father, Abut's, cave. The boy at eleven years of age should have run with the rest to the high ground. Instead he huddled in a ball in the back of the cave.

"Come out here, Boy, now," Erru ordered. Hun failed to comply, continuing to chew his nails. He appeared deaf.

Erru reached for him and dragged him out by his arm.

"What's the matter with you, Boy?" Erru demanded.

"I fear fire. I was burned once. I fear fire."

"Well, you could burn to death, if you remain here. Come with me. I have one more cave to search."

Erru held onto Hun's wrist for fear that the boy in his terror might run away to hide in some even more dangerous place. Hun's thoughts were irrational as he jumped at every sound. No other person remained behind, so Erru began the walk to the highest area nearby. He could see where the people had chosen to go. Erru's thoughts were also leaning toward the irrational as he thought it unwise that the Creator had allowed the fire to come so close to their refuge. He took Hun to Mu.

"Hang onto him," he told Mu. "He's terrified of the fire, and he could harm himself."

Maru saw the look on Hun's face and realized his terror. She knew that feeling. She ran over to him. Mu held tightly to him.

"Hun!" Maru tried to reach him, as he pulled on a fingernail sliver with his teeth, causing a finger to bleed. "Once I was as frightened as you are now. My father was killed by the bad Molgray, and I watched it happen from a tree. I had to come down that tree and run home through the forest to warn our people. I was scared of everything. One thing gave me courage."

At the word courage, Hun, who'd appeared to pay no attention at all, looked right at Maru's face.

"Hun, you're eleven years old. There are little children here, more little children here than mothers can watch. The people have a great need to watch the youngsters. The people need you this night like they needed me long ago. Hun, you have to put the needs of the people first. Shake off your thoughts enough to watch the little ones." Maru pleaded with him, for she had been watching them. It was so easy for one of them to slip away in all the confusion. Not only was a fire approaching but also snakes and large spiders and other things were crawling and creeping all over.

"Hun, the people need you!" Maru shouted over the noise of confusion and thunder, her face about a hand's length from his.

She left Hun sitting beside his mother and found Ang, his five-year-old sister, and Nug, his three-year-old cousin. She took both of them to Hun. "Now, you hold both of them," she ordered. "You are responsible for them right now. Talk to them; sing to them; tell them stories. Keep them calm. And most of all keep them with you. Don't let them wander off to be burned."

The last few words hit Hun hard. He heard all the rest but felt no commitment. Her last words brought his commitment. He could not permit the little ones to be burned. Maru, having learned to leave fear for courage, realized she had reached Hun's spirit, in a place where he finally felt, a place beyond all the terror. She went to search for children who weren't secured.

The fire approached and the rain came very heavy. The fire seemed to lose its strength a long way from the water source. Men would check on the fire from time to time. As it began to fail, they took heart but were unsure until it all seemed out.

Erru, Latap, Gol, Abut, Bid, and Fig went to the fire edge to be sure the fire was out. Besides their spears, they carried shoulder bones to scoop sand over any embers they might find. They would be at the task all night. Lamut and Perru guided the people back to their caves. Once they were in their caves, Perru and Tamin went from cave to cave to be sure all were present. They accounted for all of the people except those at the edge of the fire.

Several days later the fire was completely out; the people were all safe; the mimosa tree was safe; and way beyond their refuge the forest was half burnt. Where life had been so vibrant, it was black. Hun found Maru looking for greens for the evening meal.

"Maru, I need to talk to you."

"What is it, Hun?" Maru asked but already knew. She might be two years younger than he was, but she knew fright and courage.

"Thank you. I was terrified, and you made it so I could do something that mattered."

Maru thought for a moment. She still had bad dreams sometimes. There were times her father's face from the pole seemed to stare at her through the cloud of time. Much of that, however, was in the past. She had moved forward.

"Hun, I know what it's like to be terrified. When you feel like that, you can do something about it, or you can huddle into a ball, hoping it'll all go away, knowing it won't. The fire was a great danger. But the little ones were also in danger. There were too many for the parents to look out for. You did something courageous. You looked out for the little ones who could have been bit by spiders or snakes or bugs in the dark or burned. You helped keep them safe. Now you know what courage is."

"I wasn't courageous, Maru. I looked out for the children, the best I could, but I was terrified while I did it."

"That, Hun, is what courage is all about. Despite your fear, it's doing what needs to be done. In doing it your fear grows smaller. Could one of those little ones have wandered off?"

"Of course, they even said that they wanted to walk over to the ledge to see the fire better."

"Then look at the courage you showed. You kept them safe, when their ideas weren't."

"I think I can see what you mean. I just feel such a coward."

"Hun, when it came down to doing what was important, you were no coward. You wanted to hide in your fear, and instead you watched little ones, little ones who have no real idea what safety is. Consider that you may have saved a life. It's possible. You shook yourself out of your fear. That's like shrugging off cowardice. You are not a coward. Now you know how to overcome fear. You grew courage in place of fear."

"I suppose you're right."

"I know I am, Hun." Maru reached up and patted him on the shoulder.

She went off to gather greens, and he headed back to the refuge, where he saw Chim motioning to him. "I've been looking for you, Hun."

He looked at her.

"I struggled the night of the fire, and you took care of Mug for me. That little boy had been trying to walk by the edge of the hill to see the fire, and every time I thought I had him distracted, he'd go again. I was provoked and tired of chasing him while holding the others. Your taking care of him probably saved him, and it certainly helped me. I've made a carrying bag for you to help me say how much I appreciate your help." She handed him a rectangular bag with a flap to keep things inside. It had a strap about as wide as his thumb was long to go over his shoulder. Hun was utterly humbled.

"Thank you, Chim. It was Maru who thought to have me do that. I was terrified and she made me see beyond my terror to put in my thoughts that the people had needs. I am grateful to her. She probably should have this bag."

"Come here, Silly One," Chim said. She hugged him. "I know of Maru's participation. She learned very young how to be courageous. I also made a bag for her. No, Hun, this bag is for you—you alone."

Hun bowed his head to her. "Thank you, Chim. It's beautiful. I treasure it." And he did. Little would Chim know how much strength she added to Hun's courage for the future with the gift of that bag and the words that accompanied it.

Bid and Mat had taken a long hike to hunt the far edge of the forest. Off to the right there was a grassland that hadn't burned. They entered the grassland, saw something surprising, and quietly withdrew from it.

"What are they?" Mat asked.

"I don't know, but they're not terror birds. We should be able to eat them. Let's kill one. How about the one closest to us? It looks like the biggest," Fig said.

The two young men set up their spears and walked soundlessly into the grassy area. The rhea they had in mind was about their height. It stood on sturdy legs. It looked up, and they ran at it face on. The rheas had never seen humans. They stood fearless, watching. As their chosen bird turned to run, both sent their spears flying, and both made a direct hit. The animal was clearly wounded. Mat ran over with a rock he'd found at his feet. He grabbed the rhea by the neck and wrestled it to the ground with Fig's help. Mat hit the bird hard on the head with all his strength, and life left the bird.

They carried the huge bird home, and the men who were standing about took over the cleaning and butchering of the carcass, while others watched to see how it was done on a bird of that size. They feasted on rhea, delighting in the new flavor. Hunters would definitely strive to learn the habits and living places of the bird.

Maru climbed to the highest hill someone her age was allowed to climb. She gazed out over the expansive view around the Boqueirão refuge. It was not like the jungle where she had been a young child. It differed from the mountains she had run through. Her father's bones lay somewhere back there. But her new land was special. She loved it. In the beginning her mother, Magul, had tried to explain that her father rested with them even though his bones were elsewhere. His name was invoked every time the people performed the tree ritual. She knew the tree ritual would take place the next day. Magul told her that calling his name made it possible for him to hear in the land of the spirit, so he was close to his people even though his bones weren't close; his spirit was close. Maru stood tall and reached out her hands upward on straight arms enclosing her head, as if she were a spear. What she emulated was the leaves of the mimosa in closed position.

Holding that pose she sang her song to her father, a song no one had ever heard, "My father, Efum, wherever you may be, be with me now in this time you did not live to see. See with my eyes what I see, as I move through my days far away from your bones. Share with those we left behind that we do well here. Thank you for your gift of being my father. I keep you in my place of love." Then in her speaking voice she said, "Father, if possible, give me a sign that you hear me, when I sing my song to you and when I talk to you." Then, slowly as a mimosa tree, she separated her arms, lowering them to her sides as an opening mimosa leaf.

Maru sat there a while longer, looking out at the great view. She could see where the fire had burned part of the forest. She could see the area but not the meadow where the rhea had been found. She saw the water source. She could see Pedra Furada. Maru loved her new home. She stood, ready to return to her cave. As she reached for her spear, at the top she saw a red feather. She wondered what the red feather was doing on her spear. It was brilliant red. It must have come from a parrot flying by, she mused. Then she *knew*. The feather was from a bird flying by, no doubt, but, more than that, the feather was what she had just requested. It was acknowledgement from her father that he heard her and was with her. Red was what she associated with him because of how he died. In his death he could be there with the people. Maru knelt on the ground. She put her hands on the ground before her. She wept in old pain and new joy, tears falling straight from her eyes to the ground.

Finally, Maru stood, brushed the sand from her hands and knees, picked up her spear and the feather, and she headed home with a soul lighter than it had ever been since arrival at the Boqueirão refuge. She could still walk with her father. The spirit life that adults talked about was real. She would see her father again in the future. She *understood:* the Creator made people to last—they would change form, but they would last. The physical world folded into the spiritual world. For now she would focus on life in this time. She would turn loose of the remains of the pain, for her father was alive, and she would see him again. Maru would seek out Gol and ask him to affix the feather to her spear in remembrance that her father was close at hand.

Bibliography

G. Aimola, C. Andrade, L. Mota, F. Parenti, "Final Pleistocene and Early Holocene at Sitio do Meio, Piauí, Brazil: Stratigraphy and comparison with Pedra Furada," *Journal of Lithic Studies,* 2014, Vol 1, I 2, 5-24.

N. Guidon, G. Delibrias, "Carbon-14 dates point to man in the Americas 32,000 years ago," *Nature* 321, 19 June 1986, 769-771.

D.J. Meltzer, J.M. Adovasio, T.D. Dillehay, "On a Pleistocene human occupation at Pedra Furada, Brazil," *Antiquity,* Dec, 1994, Vol 68, Issue 261, 695-714.

F. Parenti, "Pedra Furada, Archaeology of," Istituto Italiano di Paleontologia Umana, Rome, Italy.

J.C. Santos, A.F. Barreto, K. Suguio, "Quaternary deposits in the Serra da Capivara National Park and surrounding area, southeastern Piauí state, Brazil,"

Geologia USP (December 2012), Sao Paulo, Vol 12, N 3, 115-132.

G.M. Santos, M.I. Bird, F. Parenti, L.K. Fifield, N. Guidon, P.A. Hausladen, "A revised chronology of the lowest occupation layer of Pedra Furada Rock Shelter, Piauí, Brazil: the Pleistocene peopling of the Americas," *Quaternary Science Review* 22 (2003) 2303-2310

http://www.bradshawfoundation.com/south_america/serra_da_capivara/pedra_furada/index.php

http://www.bradshawfoundation.com/south_america/serra_da_capivara/

http://www.sfu.museum/journey/an-en/postsecondaire-postsecondary/pedra_furada

http://escholarship.org/uc/item/16b81926

http://whc.unesco.org/en/list/606

https://brazilinhotpants.wordpress.com/2011/02/21/stone-wall-paintings-of-prehistoric-brazil/

Made in the USA
Middletown, DE
19 February 2017